The Honditsch Cross

Also by Ingeborg Bachmann

FROM NEW DIRECTIONS

Malina

Complete Stories (forthcoming)

Ingeborg Bachmann

The Honditsch Cross

A TALE OF 1813

Translated from the German by Tess Lewis

A NEW DIRECTIONS PAPERBOOK ORIGINAL

Originally published in Germany as *Das Honditschkreuz* by Piper Verlag in 1978.

Manufactured in the United States of America
First published as New Directions Paperbook 1630 in 2025

Library of Congress Cataloging-in-Publication Date
Names: Bachmann, Ingeborg, 1926–1973, author. | Lewis, Tess, translator.
Title: The Honditsch cross : a tale from 1813 / Ingeborg Bachmann ; [translated by Tess Lewis].
Other titles: Honditschkreuz. English
Description: New York : New Directions Publishing Corporation, 2025.
Identifiers: LCCN 2024053290 | ISBN 9780811238564 (paperback) | ISBN 9780811238571 (ebook)
Subjects: LCSH: Napoleonic Wars, 1800–1815—Campaigns—Austria—Fiction. | LCGFT: Historical fiction. | Novels.
Classification: LCC PT2603.A147 H66 2025 | DDC 833/.914—dc23/eng/20241114
LC record available at https://lccn.loc.gov/2024053290

10 9 8 7 6 5 4 3 2 1

New Directions Books are published for James Laughlin
by New Directions Publishing Corporation
80 Eighth Avenue, New York 10011

The Honditsch Cross

I

Dust whirled and enveloped the clattering wheels. The woman sitting on the wagon's narrow perch held the reins slack; dazed by the sun, she stared vacantly at her surroundings. A few drops of sweat glistened on her suntanned forehead. The woman reached for her apron and, in slow circles, wiped her roughened, angular face. Tightly framed by a black kerchief, her narrow face appeared even longer than it was. Her dark eyes were motionless and dull. It was hard to imagine any thoughts behind this forehead.

The horse was fretful, whipping its tail and wanting to prance, plagued as it was by the pesky insects, and the horseflies were biting as well.

On hot days like this, the trip from Vellach to Hermagor dragged endlessly. The dust and the pointless curves and bends in the road were so annoying that travelers longed for an end to their journey. On either side of the road's torrid, dust-ridden inhospitality, stretched the fields: those on the left, which springs made slightly marshy, grew twice as lush and vibrantly green; those on the right, by contrast, had already withered brown and yellow in the heat, which was relentless in its desire to scorch the field. The forest behind them rose in hillocks, its trees were magnificent. All this was in the distance, the Eck Forest beyond the last houses of Hermagor, and lining the road was the Ach Forest, which was now casting scant, soothing shadows.

Suddenly from behind the wagon, unsettling footsteps sounded through the wheels' monotonous clatter. The woman turned around.

"Hah," she said dismissively, "the Slovene ..."

With a single bound, the short, scrawny man drew even with the wagon, grinning agreeably.

"Nooo ..." he said, stretching the syllable indulgently. "Nooo, what do I see! Vaba Mölzer out and about. Out and about on a wagon ... And a nice one at that. Now that's something special, isn't it, a wagon of your own, hmm?"

The peddler's grin widened alarmingly. "You'll just have to lend me yours, if you have something against Kondaf's."

"Gladly. I'd be happy to, but when it comes to thanking, I'm sure you'd rather climb into Kondaf's bed than into mine," he continued taunting her, placing his hand on the prominent bulge of his pigeon breast.

Vaba Mölzer stared impassively straight ahead then let the reins drop a bit more, so that the horse picked up its pace, forcing the peddler to hobble breathlessly to keep up.

Mateh Banul—"the Slovene" to the locals—came up the Gail Valley from Villach a few times each year. Since when, no one could remember. He was somehow part of cycle of the years. The farmwives and young girls liked him and were eager to see his glittering necklaces and colorful ribbons, the farmers bought new pocketknives, screws, nails, and tools, but everyone was just as excited—or perhaps even more so—to hear his gossip and many stories about all of the nearby events. He was a master storyteller and knew how to satisfy the curiosity of the farmers who lived in such remote villages. He was no less welcome in market towns like Hermagor, since ears there were as open to chatter as anywhere. However, Mateh Banul was not Slovenian, but Windish.

The Windish live among ethnic German Austrians in the Gail Valley, as they do throughout southern Carinthia. They have their own language, which neither Slovenes nor German speakers completely understand. With their presence, they seem to want to blur the borders—the border of the country, but also of language, customs, and mores. They form a bridge, their pillars standing firmly and peacefully on both this side and the other. And it would be good if this were to remain forever the case. Their name for the Gail River is the Zila and much in their conduct is mysterious and miraculous. Their songs seem borne by a dream of vast expanses, flowing with the current of the Zila as they resound over the nearby mountains as bewitchingly as the songs of boundless Russia. In the evenings, the girls in their red skirts recline on the bank and these songs echo far beyond the willows.

It was Mateh Banul's particular conceit to refer to himself as Slovenian, wanting to be marveled at as a stranger, a rare beast. The gullible farmers' sense of marvel, however, dwindled with time, and when they learned that he was simply Windish, from near Arnoldstein, they smiled and teased him thoroughly, a treatment he disdainfully ignored and that soon became utterly boring to him. Yet for all that, he remained the Slovene.

Now he trudged alongside the cart in silence, constantly grimacing at his thin, dirty legs that tottered in huge black hobnailed shoes. The shoes had lost their shape from heavy use, just as his entire spindly figure had grown so formless that it threatened to begin clattering like a skeleton at any moment. His torso was wrapped in a tattered gray coat and a shirt, stiff with dirt, its original color no longer discernible, was visible at the neckline. His close-fitting, knee-length trousers were still relatively new, and the black fabric shone like a farmwife's Sunday best. Then his bare shins were visible, and the Slovene kept his swollen eyes fixed on their scabs. His hooked nose, as thin as the back of a knife, seemed to stick out even more prominently from his lowered head.

After a while, he quickly turned to look at the woman above him. His thin lips twitched. "Don't you want to know where I've come from?"

Her silent indifference again left him speechless for a moment, but soon he sighed with a devious look. "After such a long trip ... I'm completely wiped out today."

"Hop on then," Vaba said, annoyed. She jerked her head

unwillingly, as if she wanted to shrug off a gadfly. In the meantime, he'd already jumped onto the wagon from behind and was flailing his arms and legs, struggling to get a foothold and straining his arms to hoist the glittering merchandise, contained in two burlap sacks, onto the cart. The woman shifted to give him room on the plank. His eyes roved restlessly, peering all around until he spotted a sack beneath the plank. Then he calmly sat up straight and smoothed the beautiful black fabric of his trousers until not the slightest wrinkle remained. He reached under the plank, his hand getting slightly tangled in the woman's skirts, and pulled the sack out. It was tied in the middle with a scrap of cloth, so that the upper half drooped empty and loose onto the floorboards. Mateh Banul drilled his index finger into the tightly cinched opening and chuckled. With great effort, he fished out a few golden yellow grains, pooled them together in the palm of his hand, and tossed them in the air several times before holding them out to Vaba.

"Nooo, what do I see!" he said, looking around cautiously and furtively as if to make sure no one was watching. "You're already harvesting your maize while it's barely setting ears at the other farmers'?"

"Something wrong with that?" she asked with amazement.

"Hold on ... I'm allowed to ask. How could I have possibly thought that Kondaf still had a crop left in July when others have run out because spring is over. Well, I suppose there's rich people too."

"Won't last much longer," she tried to deflect him. "If the levies don't end either, you'll be no poorer than everyone else soon enough."

"The whole lot of you, always moaning, typical. You've already forgotten what a blessing it was that the French did away with our wretched paper money. Since we got rid of those banco notes, business is better again."

"Hah, maybe for you," she bristled. "In a situation like this, you think only of yourself. No surprise from you either, you Windish

Slovene. You don't care if they take our very last grain or not. You shake everything off like a wet dog, thinking to yourself 'as long as it doesn't affect me and I get to fill my belly.'"

"Maybe those few *Krapfen* of yours I ate were too much? Just say so and I'll think of that."

"Hunh…" she said gruffly and turned away.

"Six months ago, you weren't so tough on the Frenchies."

"I don't know about that."

"But I do."

"Well then, someone knows something."

With that, their conversation tailed off. Before long, however, Mateh Banul pulled himself together again and, undaunted, continued trying to talk to the standoffish woman. He was one of those people who feels compelled to tell others everything they've seen or heard, even the most trifling bit of information, preferably encouraged by a curious audience. But when there was no inquisitive listener urging him to unburden himself of the weight squeezing his heart, he would cast his glance around, now sadly, now with a smile, now with a sigh, until finally, asked about the cause, he would happily launch into a new tale. But with the Mölzer woman, all his cunning expressions and attempts fell flat. So he simply started in, speaking off the cuff, insistently cheerful, frequently pausing or stopping, always on the edge of his seat.

After a long, torpid winter, Villach had been prodded into a new, patriotic fervor. The most fantastical rumors made the rounds, from which one could, in good conscience, conclude that while half of the overzealous reports had been exaggerated by local chatter from the north to the deepest south of Austria, some of them contained elements of the truth. Meanwhile Austria was not immune to Prussia's successes, minor though they were. Even in Carinthia there was talk of an alliance between Berlin and Vienna, although the reaction to this news didn't come close to the one set off by the recent Tyrolean struggle for liberation. These efforts had resonated in the remotest valleys of the province, sweeping Carinthia into the maelstrom of

7

world events. The founding of the Tyrolean Landwehr, the dissemination of patriotic writings, and the activities of clandestine agitators roused their imperial Austrian neighbors, whose misfortune now seemed complete after many fruitless battles. Carinthia, on the other hand, had submitted to its fate from the beginning—not without some agitation but still with a measure of resignation. But that may be incorrect, perhaps all they lacked was a proper organization, like the one Johann Baptist Türk had valiantly led although without lasting effect. Fluctuating battles continued during the first year of occupation until the defeat at Wagram crippled all operations. One exception was the assistance provided to the Tyroleans by men of the Upper Gail Valley and the Lesach Valley. But General Broussier's measures, which held the inhabitants of Greifenburg canton—more precisely of the Kötschach-Mauthen arrondissement—accountable for their participation in the Tyrolean insurrection, caused great alarm. However, the deputies survived those days of uncertainty: to their great happiness they were dismissed without a conviction and were only required to swear a formal apology.

The winters were hard. The levies imposed a great burden on the inhabitants. Payments and raids by the enemy made them poor. They were forced to supply large quantities of bread, wine, brandy, and meat. Almost everyone eagerly awaited release from this undeserved situation.

And yet none of this came to feature in Mateh Banul's reflections. His view, although far more discerning than that of the farmers, was not quite broad either. He didn't care if the French were there or not. For him, business was always good and his feet were always tired regardless of the French, and the farmwives' cooking still awaited him, even if the pickings were slimmer than before. Well, not so much slimmer, in fact. After all, farmers don't get so poor that they can't figure out a way to get their fill. Except now, the womenfolk would shriek indignantly if he devoured a thick slice of bacon like it was nothing. So it was really all the same to him if the damned French were there or not. In fact, he even saw some advantages to their presence. He didn't have to work nearly as hard to scrape together his gossip and news. They came to him like the dust that the wind blew into his eyes, nose, and mouth along the lonely roads of his wanderings. Before it had been very difficult: what news is there to talk about and share when nothing, absolutely nothing is going on? It takes considerable imagination to whip up something exciting out of a few ridiculous scraps. The devil knows, he'd had to work hard to scrape things together. It's a terrible feeling, he often thought, that here in the nineteenth century a person has to go digging for gold in the Tauern Alps. But all these terrible feelings and all this effort, which was a challenge even for someone as clever as himself—all of this was over and done with. And it's best to think as little as possible about the unpleasant past.

At the moment, however, Mateh Banul was talking about gossip from Villach and about the stretch that he'd covered, now on foot, now hitching a ride on a cart ... The town of Sankt Paul didn't manage to deliver the last levy and supposedly General Ruska rejected their request to pay in grain or livestock ... Ha, but here's a laugh, two days ago, Liesa Matuk in Förolach got married despite her two bastards. The oldest is the mayor's ... *du maire*, he repeated to show that he also knew the foreign word ... and that dimwit Franz thinks they're both his.

At this he laughed heartily, opening his mouth much wider than necessary, and cackling so energetically that he was left gasping for air. Vaba Mölzer simply shrugged, so Mateh Banul started in again but changed his mind after just a few words and looked at her provocatively.

He'd almost forgotten the most important story. This will grab her attention: he's coming up to the first houses in Sankt Stefan, all sweaty and tired, when he sees the mail coach. But it isn't moving, so he gets closer and closer—the beast isn't budging. He gets even closer, takes a look ... one of the wheels is broken. Then he sees Tomale the driver and a gentleman standing outside, or really they're lying down or sitting half on the road .... Such a fine young gentleman, what on earth possessed him to come up here in times like these, Mateh wonders. Maybe one of those dandified Frenchmen—since all our men are away with the army or working, but not, by God, on the Gail Valley road where a guard could nab him at the next corner. That much he, Mateh Banul, had understood on first glance. Still, he wasn't some skittish farmer intimated by the world, by finely dressed gentlemen, no, he was a man used to dealing with people of every class. Despite a certain fawning obsequiousness toward richer, better situated people, and especially city folk, he wasn't intimidated by them. Especially when he didn't depend on anyone's favor or, more exactly, their money.

So, he sees this fine gentleman standing there and doesn't immediately know where to place him. He has a feeling that the man had crossed his, Mateh Banul's, path before. And now he walks up to Tomale, completely ignoring the fine gentleman, as if he had nothing to do with him, as if he wasn't even standing there, and he shakes hands with the driver, trying to talk to him. But he doesn't get very far. The fine gentleman laughs and stretches out both hands, casually, warmly, the way we do around here, like a normal person, and, as if out of sheer joy he didn't know whether to give him, Mateh Banul, a hug. At that point, it suddenly hits him: now Mateh realizes who the fine gentleman is.

The Slovene leaned far forward and turned his head to look back at the woman. He blinked at her, expecting an answer. His hands were interlocked.

"It was Franzl Brandstetter," he blurted out.

Vaba Mölzer spun around and stared at him, wide-eyed. She didn't drop the reins or make any other movement, but she was clearly shocked to the core, as if she'd been stabbed. The Slovene drank in her stupor, swallowed up her shock and savored every bit of it.

He fixed his eyes on her, watching her intently, still leaning forward with his head turned back, relishing his satisfied desire. As they stared at each other, a few words were all it took to summon the past. Powerful and close, it raged through both of their brains, the past revealed as if on a stage.

That period flooded back to her, when Vaba was still a hired girl with the Brandstetters and their only son was coming of age. No one knew exactly how or why it was that the young man had gotten so deep under her skin. Then all of a sudden Vaba had to pack up and leave the farm, with Frau Brandstetter screaming at her for the first and last time: she wasn't going to let someone like that ruin her boy, and if the boy had wanted a girl, there were better ones for him than an ugly two-bit wench like her.

Two years later, Vaba had married Mölzer, a poor cottar, who lived in a small hovel behind the buildings that lined the market square. But all of Hermagor knew that every day Vaba found some pretext to stand on the side of the square across from the church in the morning and at midday when Franz Brandstetter came and went from his lessons with the parish priest, where he learned Latin and other subjects because he wanted to study at university. She watched him arrive and followed him with her eyes as he left until he could no longer be seen. She often held a milking pail, a dustpan she would empty onto the street, or a milk can. And after Franz disappeared into the parsonage, she would stare at the object she was holding for a while, then return across the courtyard to her hovel. She kept this up until the Brandstetters sent the boy off to Vienna for a theology degree, after which he would return to his home parish to become the minister there. Mölzer died a year later. After his death, rumor had it, Vaba wasn't too particular when it came to men. Kondaf, the farmer in Obervellach, supplied her with chickenfeed year in, year out. And now and then he threw in a bit of ham and meat or cornmeal, so she wouldn't be in need. When the young women gathered and showed off to each other how very clever and knowing they were, they would laugh and sneer at her or seriously wonder what exactly men saw in this ugly, bony hag. But in fact, they knew very little about her.

Vaba Mölzer soon managed to unfreeze her expression, but it

took longer for her to regain her sense. Mateh Banul kept watching her, but he'd lost his power over her, no matter how scorchingly and insistently he stared at her. He finally looked away, then carefully and quietly sat back up. He didn't want to say another word, only to savor the situation and find out how well his jabs had landed. But he couldn't measure this from his coy side-glances; she went on sitting, impassive, as she had before.

This silent, rousing ride didn't last much longer. They'd reached the first houses of Hermagor. The Slovene looked and looked but he could only vaguely perceive what the woman's better view had already recognized. Horses crowded before the bridge that spanned the small but raging Gössering. As they approached, they saw French officers sitting astride the horses, and in their midst sat General Ruska on a large, gleaming stallion, looking small and grim as his eyes shifted this way and that. A young blond officer at his side was talking to him, he seemed to be trying to persuade him of something, emphasizing his words with gestures. The general did not look at him but abruptly let out a shrill cry, which made his horse rear. His companions drew back. Only the young, blond man stayed close behind him. Through narrowed eyes, Ruska saw the approaching cart. He looked at the few curious bystanders watching the group from a timid distance and his face flushed.

"Clear off, canaille!" he shouted and lunged forward, followed by his men, so that the gawkers quickly scattered.

Vaba Mölzer grasped the coming calamity too late and, terrified, drove the cart off the road. It came to rest with two wheels on the edge of the road and two in the marshy pasture. Miraculously, it did not tip over. The peddler clung to the rails and breathed a sigh of relief when the danger seemed to disappear behind him, vanishing in a cloud of dust. He climbed down, took his things and walked off; a few men came up, laughing as they helped Vaba pull the cart out of the mud.

II

In the large, cool room of the rectory, Father Freneau sat in an armchair at his desk. He hummed absentmindedly with his head bowed, his hands flat on his stomach, lost in vague musings with no particular direction. This beneficial rest quieted all the stirrings of body and mind, so he was annoyed when the creak of the door announced a visitor. He turned and peered into the darkness in front of the newly closed door, blinking his eyes several times. Then he gasped and leapt up, almost overturning his chair. "Good Lord if it isn't ... Well I'll be ... it is ... Welcome home, Master Studiosus!"

In a flash he was at the young man's side, taking his hands and shaking them over and over.

"We won't let you get away any time soon, Master Studiosus. Now what you need is a proper vacation. After three years, it's time to be home a while!"

Then Freneau fell silent and the young man, laughing, let himself be led to the window. Freneau pulled a chair from the side table and drew it up to the desk. They sat for a while in silence, then Franz Brandstetter again took both of the priest's hands and said with a deep breath, "Greetings, Dean Freneau, *Grüss Gott!*"

"My, my," the priest murmured and looked at the floor, glancing up shyly a few times at his visitor. "He's all grown up, our little Franzl is, a proper gentleman," he said, pulling himself together.

Now Brandstetter laughed with relief because an unpleasant, disconcerting tension had passed between them.

"But Father, I learned my first Latin words with you and got my last good clip on the ear—so I can stay the boy I was. Of course you should still call me Franzl."

"But that's not proper ..."

"For goodness' sake, what next. If I say that's how it is, then that's how it'll be."

The priest straightened up and became animated again. "Well, Franzl, to be honest, I prefer it too. For me, you're still that boy, a very clever boy, but still a boy. Change is hard for an old man."

The ice was now broken, and a lively exchange of stories and questions followed. Old Freneau became jolly and so relaxed that the residents of Hermagor would have been astonished to see the stern cleric in such a jovial mood—especially when, after the hardships of recent years, he often harangued his flock venomously from the pulpit, at least that's what his parishioners said. But they didn't understand his true nature, nothing really grated on his nerves enough to truly anger or upset him. Rather, he possessed a certain superior haughtiness, and his creatively clever irony often left the farmers shaking their heads. He kept his distance, never seeking closer ties, so it was extraordinary how fond he had become of the young Brandstetter and with how much pride he looked at his former student. He had a sense that this young man was his handiwork, his creation, and that all Franz's admirable talents were things he had impressed upon the boy. In the end, he bound his own longings—whether vague or concrete—to Franz Brandstetter's existence, and expected that he would achieve in him the fulfilment of all that was missing from his own life. The boy's decision to study theology years before had felt like a wave of happiness breaking over his life and truly nothing, however desirable, could have meant more to him.

Brandstetter had to tell him all about Vienna and the reverend father dredged up experiences from his own student years, humorous and rambunctious things he'd all but completely forgotten, which he never had enough leisure nor enough joy in his life to recall. The hour they shared seemed to him the product of some fantastic enchantment: such a pleasant, comfortable, unstructured companionship with a lively young man who reminded him of his own younger self, which had long since been shackled to the routines of work. That earlier self hadn't died, yet it was powerless to suppress the inner unrest that had fashioned this man's idiosyncrasies into an outlook on life that was truly his own.

Suddenly, Freneau broke off. His eyes gleamed, still a little watery with joyful excitement. "Tell me, Franzl, I've forgotten the most important thing. How did you manage to get here? From Vienna, from the seat of the Empire to the territory under French control? You'll have to tell me. Good Lord, my boy, you couldn't have just up and left, and I can't believe that the French are so stupid they didn't catch you anywhere on the long stretch to Hermagor."

"Of course, I wasn't that careless. A colleague of mine, whose father is an important politician in the Vienna court, obtained a *lettre de permission* from the French civil administration in Laibach for the *Province illyrienne de Carinthie*, in other words, our Villach region. With this border pass, I made it home unhampered, except for a few checks."

"Aha, that was very clever of you. And on top of that, you were one lucky devil. Not everyone has a friend with high connections, much less one who's willing to share them. I have yet to hear of a single case where someone from outside made it here, to us, or the reverse."

"Honestly, Reverend Father, it wouldn't have occurred to me. I've always hoped to make it home, but not this way. My colleagues and I wanted to join the Archduke Karl's army as soon as possible. It was very hard for us, just having to watch and listen while others were allowed to fight—they wouldn't let us theologians take part in it anywhere! And if we all rallied together we might even manage to free the Gail Valley!"

Gushing like an impulsive child, he was completely swept up in the idea.

"But Franzl, Franzl, you want to be a theologian. Dear boy, you should all use your swords to preach peace. Leave waging war to the others," Freneau exclaimed cheerfully. For the first time, he was struck by the new tone with which they spoke. It pleased him.

Brandstetter lowered his head slightly and blushed. "Yes, but I mean, my desire to join the fight can't be much of a surprise. Every young person, theologian or not, finds joy in that. Especially now, when you're not even allowed to come home for a few years because of the French …"

He gave the priest a slightly inquiring look. The latter simply shook his head, so Franz continued, "And hasn't Praskowitz himself taken command of everyone?"

At this Freneau started up. "So you've heard about that too. Yes, you know, my dear fellow clergyman from Sankt Leonhard always was hot-blooded. Especially now! He can't stand it when young fellows set up secret organizations, he demands to be the first, and when they helped people in Tyrol and the Lesach Valley three years ago, he dispensed the guns and ammunition and delivered fiery propaganda from the pulpit."

"I don't know if that's the worst thing for our people. It's better for their priest to lead them. Left on their own, they might be stupid enough to do something unjustifiable and end up in a situation they should have been spared."

"Well, about their stupidity, I'm not convinced. The farmers aren't as stupid as they pretend to be or as they appear. In my opinion they've even developed some incredible talents and pack a harder punch than the gents from cadet schools. What they lack in skill, they make up for with strength and vigor. But as for Praskowitz and his views on the role of the clergy, I strongly disagree."

Freneau paused briefly. He touched his tongue to his lips as if hesitating. The student didn't notice. Then Freneau continued, now more deliberately, "Wouldn't you rather leave the guns to the soldiers? They're the ones suited to fight wars. I have nothing against this, I truly don't, because I've realized that it's just the way of the world and even in the most pious eras, men can't live without conflict. Much as I wish it were otherwise."

Brandstetter lowered his eyes, somewhat at a loss, disappointed by the one person he'd hoped would understand him. On the other hand, he felt very close to the priest and was moved by all kinds of emotions.

"Franz," the priest's voice roused him, now more stern, "you're not going to disappoint me, are you? Tell me, are your studies already too much for you, do you need a break because you have doubts or are you truly unable to embrace them because something is hindering you, maybe because you ..."

"No, no, what are you thinking, Father?" the young man cried, clasping his fingers together. "I still love theology as much as I did when I left, I really do. And to someday take over your position, which I hope to God you'll hold for a long time yet, is my highest wish, just as it is yours. But if I've said or thought something foolish in passing ... you mustn't take it seriously ... I didn't mean it seriously myself."

"As long as you're honest with yourself," Freneau replied.

"No, no, Reverend Father, you can believe me. All these new ideas, the disbelief that's spreading everywhere, questioning the old ways, none of it has changed me. I have no room for it, and on the rare occasions when doubts have crept in, I condemned and banished them. Honestly ... I would never want to serve in Vienna or any other city, even in a university city, only here, where everything is still so unspoiled and the way it always was, where I know people and they know me. That will be both my finest calling and my vocation ..."

Brandstetter was agitated and he kept searching for words. He tried to make sense of the thoughts that came rushing at him like a thundering waterfall. A peculiar fear insinuated itself in him and he wanted to leap up and dash to the window, open it, and let some sunlight into the dreary room. A thought suddenly occurred to him: Why did Freneau have such odd doubts about his resolve and what led Freneau from the start to challenge his feelings so stubbornly? He cast about among all possible answers and finally decided that, if anything, a woman could be a stumbling block that could cause him to falter. He breathed a sigh of relief, dropped his reserve, and fixed his gaze on the priest, eyes wide open. Then he smiled. "No, nothing is hindering me."

Freneau was surprised but he understood right away. In an indulgent, sympathetic tone, he said, "Then everything is fine."

He'd had a different concern. He stood up and looked out the window.

"I never notice anymore how lovely it is outside. Come, let's take a little walk."

He chuckled to himself at how touched he'd been by the student and how differently, how obligingly he'd treated him. It was completely unlike him, but no harm was done.

III

It was still before nightfall when the student Franz Brandstetter entered Jakob Unterberger's inn. Even so, all the tables in the large public room were full and he was met with a furious babble of voices. The long tables were occupied by French soldiers and to their left stood a special table covered with a white tablecloth. This was set for the officers and in their midst sat General Ruska. Dusty and parched, they'd just arrived from Sankt Stefan, under Ruska's personal command. The residents of Sankt Stefan had once again failed to deliver their levy in time, more precisely, they couldn't for the life of them come up with the required amounts of grain and brandy. It had been due five days earlier and so, when the general's rage had boiled over, he trotted there himself at noon and held a tribunal.

There was a considerable clamor. The thirsty men had quickly downed a few glasses and were already carrying on loudly even though it was still early. The general emptied his glass in one swallow and stared blankly ahead while fidgeting with the empty glass.

The innkeeper Jakob Unterberger leaned against the door, ready to fulfill his guests' wishes at a moment's notice. On the table next to him stood a half-empty beer glass, which he grabbed in passing for a swig. He quickly wiped the foam from his moustache and blissfully closed his deep-set eyes.

Brandstetter scanned the room, and when he spotted a few locals in back, almost all of whom had been his school classmates, he quickly joined them.

Naturally they recognized Franz right away, and thanks to Mateh Banul, rumors of his arrival has spread more rapidly than if it had been announced at the market. Some simply stared at the table, a few curious ones looked in his direction. But Brandstetter's open friendliness prevented any estrangement from setting in. "*Grüss Gott*, everyone!" he called out, laughing as he gave each of them his hand, which they now could not clasp fast enough. They shifted to make room and pulled up a chair.

Although their conversation had stalled, Kaspar Unterberger, the innkeeper's son, was not shy. "Well, you sure were away a long time."

"I'd say," Irg Möderndorfer added.

"I'm glad to be back home. Vienna's nice too, but I definitely won't stay away this long again. I see you're all in good form, but now you have to tell me what's going on and what you've been doing this whole time."

"My God, just work, nothing new," Irg grinned.

"Not a very clever question on my part," Brandstetter laughed in reply. "But that's not how I meant it. You know what I'm asking."

"Hmm," Stoffel Pirker grunted, and they all fell silent. The student had the feeling of being excluded from a secret of some kind. As if they were all unable to trust him fully. So, he'd become a stranger to them, and whatever they'd been discussing among themselves, they weren't going to share it with him. Because he was sitting right there and none of them knew how or in what capacity he'd returned home. He wanted to tell them that he was still the same person, that they should act the same as they had back then, when he went along with them wherever they went. But a painful bitterness made him choke on his words. Their silence upset him more than he'd wished, and he found it hard to breathe. The tobacco smoke that filled the room tickled his throat. He felt very peculiar. He half closed his eyes and pressed his lips together. He felt an enormous pressure in his head and thought his temples might burst. He suddenly felt like every part of him—eyes, mouth, and limbs—was filling up with something menacing, perhaps hatred, and because he was so wounded he was on the verge of doing something terrible. He rubbed his fists together and felt the blood throbbing in his veins. The others sat there dully, too far from him to see these barely noticeable signs of aching aggrievement. Only the silence made them ill at ease and they were so spellbound by it that they couldn't even reach for their glasses to wash away its harshness. The foreign sound of the talk intruded from the next room. At that moment Jakob Unterberger entered and approached their table, laughing broadly. He pulled the disconcerted Brandstetter from his dangerous train of thought, and at the same time literally lifted him off his chair.

"Franzl Brandstetter, I can't believe I didn't see you right away. But with so much work ... You see how things are here. Come with me to the kitchen for a moment. The family wants to see you and get a whiff of that foreign air."

"I'll be back in a bit," Brandstetter said hoarsely and followed the innkeeper. Together they crossed both rooms and stepped into the corridor.

Just then, a peering face vanished from the crack in the kitchen door. It was Fini, the waitress, a distant relative of Jakob Unterberger who'd been taken in as a young girl and had initially helped out in the kitchen and the stable. In time, she also began serving beer and wine and ultimately became a proper waitress who now even chatted with the guests. Jakob Unterberger had nothing against this. He knew how many more customers a young, blossoming creature will attract, and he liked the sight of her. On top of that, she was a quick learner, nimble, and energetic.

When Fini saw Franz Brandstetter enter the premises, she quickly slipped into the kitchen. She didn't want to meet him in front of others in the public room, and instead she waited in the hope that he'd soon appear in the kitchen. She put on a clean apron and fussed with her hair, straightening her braids. Then she aimlessly set out a few glasses, put them away, and picked up a dish towel. She wound the dish towel wistfully around her finger, and unwound it again.

Jakob Unterberger came into the kitchen with his wife, Lisa, and with his arms raised announced what Fini had already seen. Namely, that Franz Brandstetter, who was studying to become a priest in Vienna, had stopped in, and he was going to fetch him right away. Lisa didn't object, she was also much too curious, but this weakness did not prevent her—as it did Fini—from working calmly.

"Fini, please, stop standing around. I think the general is already screaming again," she said, stirring the porridge with one hand and taking the milk that was boiling over off the flame with the other.

Fini, who otherwise was not easily detained didn't budge and simply answered, "So he can wait a while longer."

The innkeeper's wife made herself busy in the kitchen, and after a moment said, "Fini, please go. Do me a favor, otherwise he'll throw another of his unbearable tantrums and smash half my glasses against the wall."

But Fini missed the end of her sentence. She heard more steps and rushed to the door—and it really was Franz. But she didn't go out right away. Feigning indifference, she picked up a few dirty pots and put them in the sink.

Franz Brandstetter appeared and went up to Lisa Unterberger with a friendly smile. There was the usual astonishment—brief questions about his travels and his time in Vienna—and Brandstetter said flatteringly to her that despite the hard times she was still a pretty, plump person, upon which she laughed even louder than usual. Then he turned away because the young woman was still there.

"It's Fini if I'm not mistaken," he said in a playfully inquisitive tone.

"It sure is," she laughed and offered her hand, "you really didn't recognize me?"

"I almost didn't," he laughed too, "you've grown so much in the meantime ..." Now he noticed her radiant young face, her lively brown eyes, framed by dark, gleaming hair. "And, well, you know what I mean."

"Sure, I know what you mean." She withdrew her hand.

At that instant, the door was kicked open.

"Hello there, waitress!" Smiling, a young blond officer, the same one who'd been at General Ruska's side at midday, entered the kitchen. His steps were heavy and determined, like those of someone who's drunk. Everyone turned toward him and Fini quickly called out, "I'll be right there, Hauptmann, sir."

"Not good enough, sweetheart." He put his hands on her hips. "Come right now. The general's order is an order."

Fini was a master of such situations and others besides. She wasn't brusque or rude, no, that wouldn't have worked with the foreign soldiers who were the victors here, and who took full advantage of it. She was clever, laughed, joked a bit and nimbly escaped the drunken men's lustful attentions. Despite the inebriation and vulgarities of the evening shift, she was still wholesome, even if there was no room left for primness and her sense of shame was blunted. Still, with Brandstetter's disconcerting eyes on her, Maroni's harmless gesture made the blood rush to her head.

"Let go of me," she said, annoyed, and jerked free. Maroni was in too good a mood to notice that she was serious. He reached for her arm, attempting to caress it.

"But Fini ..." he tripped over his tongue. She lashed her arm at him and strode toward the door with her head thrown back. The captain hesitated, his smile vanished, and he followed her out, confused by his emotions.

Jakob Unterberger started to speak but stopped and, perplexed, looked at Franz Brandstetter. There was consternation on every face. The student said a few disjointed words. "How quickly the first day goes by ..." He felt laughter rising inside him and took pains to control himself. "Please don't be annoyed with me that I've stopped by on my first evening."

"Of course not," Lisa Unterberger said, excited. "We understand how things are. As happy as we are to see you, you should spend your first day at home. You must've been a sight for your mother and father, showing up like this without warning—no letter, no message."

"You'd already heard too?" Brandstetter said, cheering up. "It seems like everyone knew even before I did."

"Could be," she said with a low, booming laugh.

Unterberger had begun setting glasses in a tub to wash them while Lisa rushed back and forth. Brandstetter felt quite useless and made an effort to speak, which Lisa answered with a laugh or an occasional interjection as she bustled about. When Stoffel Pirker—why is unclear, but certainly not because of him—sauntered down the corridor, Franz made a quick end to the conversation and said that they were waiting for him in the back room. "I'll be seeing you."

And with that Brandstetter was out of the kitchen.

In the corridor, he again felt his face flush with all the memories. No, he couldn't return so quickly. He turned away, shyly, and stepped quietly into the courtyard. The modest patch of ground was enclosed on all four sides, a peculiar building style that was rare in Carinthia. The twilight masked the dirt and clutter, but Brandstetter nonetheless felt as if the filth was something creeping up to him, very close and disgusting. In one corner, right next to the smaller living quarters, lay the dung heap, over which danced the swarms of mosquitos it attracted. Near it was the door to the stable. The faint gleam of a cigarette caught his eye and faded amid the messily scattered straw. Horses, several of which were tied in the courtyard near the wall and kept outside, stamped restively. A woman, probably the stable maid, let out a squeal, then he heard giggling, and then it was quiet again. Franz Brandstetter felt a sense of freedom. He was removed from these people who knew nothing beyond their own aches and pains. He took a deep breath, swatted at the mosquitos, and was about fall prey to the gloom that comes from feeling misunderstood. Then he thought of Freneau again and how he had tried to convince himself—how pathetic he now felt! It was true, after all, that he'd recently had more and more doubts about his calling, less because of a lack of faith than from the prevalence of other interests. For the new commotion in his fatherland had caught hold of him more powerfully than anything ever had before.

And yet at times he questioned whether this desire to escape the shackles of his predetermined future was really authentic. But these doubts were immediately displaced by a painful awareness of the truth of his intentions: a thousand times he struggled to subdue this awareness, only to passionately embrace it just as often. He would then curse his life because he didn't know how to take hold of it, to be guided by some firm resolution, one that was for him an inner law. In his anguish, he often thought that some law stemming from the divine sense of purpose that all healthy people—of which he was one, for Heaven's sake—either have or should have as a driving force, would suddenly make him open his mouth and shout, This is what I want!

He certainly wanted many different things, he thought. But less than wanting something specific, this was more of a vague longing—and for this longing he chided himself as a capricious child who didn't know what he could torment himself with most. With the fading day, these realizations again began to loom inside him. Then a strange delirium released him from this thrall—a craving for freedom or some similar euphoria. He sighed with relief. Jolted from his rapture by the sound of someone stretching nearby, Brandstetter looked over to see a French soldier, the stable boy who slept near the horses, sitting up. The boy had heard his comrades tramping in from the street through the narrow gap that separated the stables from the living quarters.

"A lummox," the stable boy grinned at them and pointed at Brandstetter who staggered backward into the house.

"How? ... What?" two of them asked.

"Nothing," he turned around and winked. "Did you ... ? Ahh, well done!" He uncorked the bottle with boyish delight as the others stretched out next to him. As the older stable maid came out of the stall, slipped off her wooden shoes, and shuffled toward the house with a pail of milk, the stable boy quickly took a gulp from the bottle, rested his head against the wall, and began to sing, melting into his companions' laughter:

... rien d'argent, rien du tout.
Rien qu'une petite comme toi
À taille svelte ...

He burped, laughing, broke off his singing, and finally lifted the bottle properly. Meanwhile the woman had disappeared into the house.

At around midnight the liveliness inside had reached its peak, as it did in the back room, where Franz Brandstetter had long since rejoined the others. All of them, Franz included, were in a good mood and no longer completely sober, although quite innocuous compared to the French who were so drunk they no longer knew if they were strolling along the boulevards in Paris or practicing tightrope walking on the tables at Jakob Unterberger's in Hermagor. Tables and floor were wet with spilled beer, wine, and brandy. The tobacco smoke had thinned somewhat since almost none of them were even capable of bringing their cigars or pipes to their lips. The young men in the back room gleefully observed this unholy chaos. Brandstetter was speaking, and the conversation turned to Dean Freneau.

"... this morning I visited him right away. You can imagine how wide he opened his eyes and mouth ..."

The student didn't notice the sudden disenchantment that spread over all the faces at these words. One-eyed Hans Irg angrily exclaimed from the corner, "The Frenchmen's Alsatian servant."

Brandstetter didn't even hear the interjection. He emptied his glass and grinned. Then he glanced over at the French. "Such fine gentlemen, eh?" he laughed. Then upon reflection he added, "But tell me, are you not allowed to sit with them? Do you have to stay in the back room?"

The innkeeper's son leaned forward furtively. "Maybe you'd like to join them?"

"Certainly not at the moment. They're capable of bashing our heads with a beer mug."

"But if they weren't drunk, then it would be fine?" Kaspar retorted pointedly.

"What do you mean, *fine?*" the student laughed and waved to the innkeeper.

Unterberger poured another round, yawned, and grumbled about his weak knees.

"The French are very nice people. I like them well enough," Pirker observed innocently.

"What's that?" Brandstetter exclaimed. "I've heard they're not exactly gentle with us—and yet you still like them. What a joke. A fine man, Stoffel is. He sympathizes with the French. What do you all say to that?"

He slammed the table with his hand. The others hid their smiles and nudged each other without taking their eyes off him. They'd sobered up. Now Brandstetter had to show his colors and let them know where he stood.

"Hmm ..." Kaspar paused, "We don't say anything. Nowadays, it's better we keep our mouths shut. It would be best for you if you did the same. You're shouting your opinions at the top of your lungs. If one of them understands what you're saying, you'll have a bad day tomorrow."

Brandstetter was stunned. He'd never expected this. He didn't know what to say. Should he retreat or keep going ... He began tentatively, "Yes, but ... I don't understand you all ... And anyway, if I really had been shouting, they couldn't have heard what I was saying, they're so smashed ... Besides, that's not how I meant it at all ..."

His embarrassment convinced the lads. He wasn't posturing and the fact he wanted to take it back was proof enough for them of what he had meant. Kaspar Unterberger gave a loud, resounding laugh. "Cheers, boys. Franzl is one of us. We won."

The student was astonished, then furious, and he shouted, "What the hell is that supposed to mean? You think I'm playing the fool?

You can carry on, for all I care, but leave me in peace. Go ahead, report me if you want. Maybe they'll give you a medal or a bag of money. But the Judas should tell me to my face if he's not too much of a coward. I'd like to know who he is."

He sprang up and glowered threateningly behind his chair.

The situation had become serious—this was clear on every face. Fini threw timid glances into the room and would have liked to know what was going on so she could step in to mediate, but she couldn't hear what was happening over the rest of the noise. And now that she was sitting next to the general, it was impossible to get away.

Kaspar Unterberger did the smartest thing he could. He stood up, too, and laid a hand on Franz's shoulder. "Sit down, Franzl, I'll explain everything. I'm sure you think you're in a madhouse." He pulled him back onto his chair. "Listen. Here's the story. You come all the way from Vienna to us at home. You're so close to Father Freneau that we had no way of knowing how things stood with you. Do you want to know more from us or not? Do you care what's happening here or not? And most important, are you with the French or with us? If we asked a stupid question earlier, right, you can't take it seriously. But your answers told us that you're angry with the French, that you'd want to see them gone immediately. We're glad and we'll talk more tomorrow in the light of day."

The student said nothing, then burst out like before. "Aha, so that's how it is with all of you—and you take me for such a lowlife."

"That's enough," one-eyed Irg ordered. "Be honest, what were we supposed to do, do you think we're stupid, that we're going ride straight into a disaster and tell you plainly where we stand?"

Brandstetter didn't respond; he had to come to terms with the situation. The sting wasn't entirely gone, but as he mulled it over, he admitted that they'd had no choice.

Kaspar left the group with a secretive wink and soon returned with something hidden under a towel. He licked his lips and, after a silent, conjuring gesture with his hand, lifted the cloth. A bottle of wine! They all cheered enthusiastically. It was good to have the innkeeper's son as a friend.

For two years, all the wine had flowed to the occupying army and possession of this coveted beverage brought severe penalties. Jakob Unterberger managed the stores of wine and brandy and by law was prohibited from taking even so much as a drop for himself or for anyone from the civilian population. But it's a rare innkeeper who isn't sly enough to find his way around the rules and still have his daily glass or more and sometimes pass a bottle around his circle of friends. Unterberger did this with particular delight because it meant putting one over on the French who were keeping half their horses in his stables and had quartered a dozen soldiers in his home.

Finally, when the new day dawned, the young men dispersed. A brief goodbye to the innkeeper and to Fini, along with their thanks for the good wine, dispersed like a haze. Kaspar Unterberger left as well, accompanying them part of the way. Taking in the fresh night air, they felt lighter and, yawning, they each made their separate way home.

Tired and worn out, Fini again sat on the bench next to the general. Fortunately, he would fall into gloomy spells every so often and leave her alone for a bit. The others were easier to shake off. Beyond the exhaustion, today she felt a bitter aversion to the men around her, a rage was welling up inside her. Never before had her work filled her with so much awareness—and hatred—of the filth and nastiness surrounding her. She couldn't explain this clear-sightedness. Every time she thought of Franz Brandstetter, she cursed the French, the wine, and the inn—she would've preferred ten times over to be a farm girl. That would mean having to work all day and the food wouldn't be as good as it was here, but no one would be allowed to paw at her however he wanted, and she would never be forced to sit there, tired and sleepy, because someone wanted her to and chose to stay even longer.

One of the soldiers started to sing a song that drowned out the clamor. Young Maroni, already half-asleep, perked up, came around the table, and with a groan shoved aside a few slouching officers who had trouble staying in their chairs and could not defend themselves. He squeezed in next to the waitress. "Paulette, little Paulette, what's come between us? Don't be so angry. Paulette ... ette ..." He put his hand on her shoulder.

Indifferent, Fini scooted away and kept her eyes straight ahead.

Hauptmann Relioz, aside from the general, was the oldest soldier there. He slammed an old pewter tankard he'd gotten hold of on the table. "Silence, damn it!"

Even the general was startled and gave Relioz an astonished glance. The captain didn't notice and instead began laughing boisterously. The long, wide scar disfiguring his nose and one of his cheeks swelled up and turned bluish red, making him an ugly, even repulsive sight. In contrast to his face, however, his body was well proportioned and well trained, and he was the best rider of them all.

Once again he slammed down the tankard, with less force this time, and it slipped from his fingers in front of a young lieutenant, who glared at him, shocked by the violent interruption. With more verve than veracity he'd been recounting hair-raising events from his time in Paris in elaborate detail. He'd held the group's rapt attention, but Relioz had a sudden idea and would tolerate no voice but his own.

"Comrades," he rasped across the table, "Comrades, it's all nonsense. Nonsense, all of it. The young man wants to tell you stories. This is nothing to laugh at. A man that young couldn't have had a fraction of those experiences. Who didn't know Leutnant Relioz in Paris? I was still a lieutenant at the time. Every woman knew me. They stared at me with eyes aflame, they turned their heads and ran after me, a few even came to my room, hah, what am I saying? A dozen, two dozen. I didn't have time to count all of them. Each was prettier than the last. But then there was a countess or something, high nobility, an old family, the little doll had been in Austria in 1789, so she'd kept her proud head. Would've been a shame if she'd lost it ... What was I saying? Yes, she was a countess with a long line of ancestors and more aristocratic arrogance than was really necessary. Naturally she didn't even notice me. You know how it is. And I didn't see her. But, when I did take a look at her I thought to myself, this one is worth it. Make an effort, Leutnant Relioz, you old, young gallant, you. When she walked—she liked to wear fine white silk—ah, her dress clung to her so wonderfully when she walked ... Nonsense, I'm not going to start gushing about the woman. In short, she didn't need to undress, I could see it all, her dress might as well have been see-through. Which doesn't mean," he pounded the table with his fist and laughed, "that it was enough for me."

Now everyone burst into laughter, shaking with amusement at such childish talk. They were happy to believe what they were hearing. One of them, a quiet person who'd become incredibly drunk, staggered up, then bent over the table and vomited.

"Pig!" the general roared and leapt from his seat. Turmoil set in. A few soldiers snapped to attention, a few others laughed, rounded their backs, howling so that the sounds they made no longer resembled anything like human voices.

Fini went pale at both horrors and thought that she should go fetch a rag. But Ruska grabbed her arm roughly. "Come Fini, we're going to the back room!"

She shuddered. "What would the General like to drink?" she asked, trying to deflect him, and walked to the door with him.

"*Un petit verre.* One for you too, otherwise you're too gloomy, little one."

"I'll be right there," she replied and walked slowly down the corridor.

Two arms held her tight.

"Pfah!" she gasped, frightened to death, trying to push him away.

"But Fini!" Kaspar's voice calmed her. She freed herself and went into the empty kitchen, followed by his heavy steps.

"But Fini," Kaspar began sheepishly and stepped in front of her. He saw that her eyes were filled with tears. She turned away quickly. He didn't know what to say, so he started blustering, half helplessly, half reproachfully. "Now that's the kind of girl I like. You barely touch her and she's all tears. God only knows what had been done to her." He cleared his throat and looked at her back. "Now that's what I like. Turning away and acting offended. You're not saying anything because you don't know what to say."

At these words, she spun around with a sob. "No one leaves me alone. Everyone thinks he can wipe his fingers on me. With you, I always thought you were a decent one, all these years we got along, and now you want to start in, too. It makes me sick. I just want to spit!" After a moment of silence, she began again. "There's not a single person who's even a little nice to me! Everybody just adds one more obstacle in my way."

She dropped onto a chair. Any other time, Kaspar Unterberger would've grinned and presented himself as the one person who wanted to be very nice to her. Today he saw her despair and how serious she was—Fini, who was otherwise unfailingly cheerful—and his mood was far from merry.

"Fini," he went over to her, "be sensible. That's not at all how I meant it. I've just had a little to drink—don't hold it against me. You're tired, too. Lie down and rest, that would be best for you. I'll stay up and take care of the bums."

She wiped her eyes with the dish towel and gave him a friendlier look.

"Would that be all right?" he asked again.

She nodded. "That's nice of you. I really would like to go bed now ... Jesus!" She jumped up and ran to the door. "The general!"

She yanked open the door, hoping to lessen the general's jealousy a little, but she then ran right into him. Ruska took a step back then pulled the door open even wider.

"Hah!" He bit his lip and gave the young Unterberger a nasty look. He pulled Fini violently to him. He raged. "*Charogne*, hussy, am I supposed to wait even longer because you're flirting with this rascal!"

The rest of his words were lost in a flood of ranting and raving. Finally, he was reduced to croaking in a shrill tone, "*Au diable, diable!*"

But Fini was no longer in reach. She'd made her escape in the corridor. Ruska contained himself, turned around without a word, and found her there, sitting on a small barrel in the dark. He was now completely gentle, he dropped on one knee before her and started begging and flattering her. "But Fini, but Fini, *ma petite*, you can't make a fool of me, the great General Ruska, in front of the scoundrels. Five minutes, just five more minutes. You can't make a fool of me like that."

He stroked her hands. Finally, she stood up without a word, and went into the back room with him, making a point of bringing a lantern. Followed by Ruska's eyes, she silently fetched the brandy, poured him a glass, and stayed near him. At first, he wanted to force her to drink, but he yielded to her unusually stern demeanor. After a few minutes, she stood up resolutely. The look in his eyes revealed his intentions, so she refused to be kept there any longer. He couldn't remain seated at the table alone. He stood up as well and started pacing back and forth.

Fini walked quickly down the corridor, softly calling good night to Kaspar. She stepped into the courtyard, and crossed it to reach the outdoor staircase on the building opposite leading up to her room. Halfway up she turned around, went down to the well, and dipped her cupped hands into the water. She drank a cool swallow and with a second handful washed her flushed face. She thought for a moment, then went back in the house and into the kitchen, to get something she'd forgotten. After a while she shuffled back, exhausted. The splash of the well and the faint whisper of the laughing soldiers inside filled her ears. The night was moonless but not dark, just mild and blue like the sea. It was easy to make out faces at a short distance, and pale skin and white clothes gave one away.

She stepped onto the creaking wooden staircase, climbed up a few steps and stopped. She'd been completely lost in thought, but looked up when she paused. Her frightened eyes took in the dark shadow, the black figure pressed against the wall above her. She hadn't yet recognized the man, but somehow she knew it was the general. She wasn't sure what to do, but she grasped the situation and what was waiting for her. In that instant, a crowd of thoughts rampaged through her mind. It was too late for anything. Her gesture of flight set Ruska in motion and he closed the gap between them with a single leap. Fini was unable to make a sound. A mute struggle kept the two suspended—the woman in fear, the man in desire. He dragged her up the stairs and she felt limp. All her fear and horror again welled up inside her, but she managed to gain a foothold and pushed the man away.

She nearly fell, but suddenly felt freed, and, reeling, she heard a dull thud.

Unable to steady himself, Ruska had taken an unfortunate tumble and now lay—just for a few seconds—curled up in the muck of the dung heap, which had seeped from the untidy pile in a wide arc all the way to the foot of the stairs.

At the sound of the heavy body's fall, a few soldiers had hurried over with a lantern, with which they illuminated the general. He leapt to his feet as if he'd been bitten, although the pain in his lower back was so sharp that he couldn't stand up straight. He raved like an epileptic, woke everyone with his shouting, and the officers along with the innkeeper and his family who came rushing out of the buildings had to sober up quickly. Fini stood there spellbound, watching the scene unfold, not knowing if this outcome was better or if it would wind up being twice as bad when all was said and done. The soldiers glanced from the general to her and back, quickly drew their own conclusions, and were barely able to suppress their gloating smirks.

IV

When you leave the ugly inner courtyards in Hermagor, it's a pleasure to open your eyes. A body of water—a quiet little brook draped with slender stalked grasses and all types of foliage, its banks dotted with rare marsh marigolds—marks a border between the mundanity of the market town and the marvelous solitude of the town's surroundings.

Franz Brandstetter was traipsing across the meadow. His shoes were already damp from the moist ground, but he didn't notice because his eyes were fixed on the forests, which were thicker than in many another place. They were beautiful and had only been lightly logged. The student found this deeply gratifying, even if he was also forced to think of how the French had long planned to put an end to this abundance of trees. He headed toward the dark forest, entered it, and let its shade dry the sweat from his sunbaked brow. From deep within came the sound of branches cracking, and the voices he'd heard earlier disappeared in the dense woods. The villagers had to start gathering wood during the summer. Previously, before these hard years, they'd been well-off and warmed their homes with wood they either harvested from their own land or bought. Today they looked back on those winters as the good old times, and every day they wished for the return of this blissful time.

The parish church bell tolled twelve times and the student turned toward home. He didn't leave the forest but followed a shortcut of his own. He was practically trotting home because his mother wouldn't stand for anyone missing from table.

Franz stopped in front of the Mölzer woman's cottage, from there, if he skirted it, he could reach the main road.

Vaba was outside, washing laundry in a tub on the bench. She turned to see who was coming, standing very erect, her arms hanging by her side. Franz was torn. He wanted to go home, but there was no way to avoid saying hello. Vaba dried her hand and offered it to him, looking through him stiffly.

Past events, although long dead, made Franz uncertain. Their conversation was perfunctory, more precisely, he talked while she nodded, her eyes closed. Finally, he said that his mother was waiting with lunch. "Goodbye, then!"

She peered straight at him and the look in her black eyes, as desolate as gloom itself but still flickering with distant light, made him feel helpless and shy. He hurried off in a state of agitation.

This, however, was one of those days when everyone had to cross his path. Mateh Banul was dragging his leg more than usual, making genuinely doleful faces and calling to Franz that he could feel a storm coming …

For God's sake, let there be a storm, he didn't care, the student thought, annoyed. Then up drew Freneau's two-horse carriage with its liveried driver. And then, to add to Franz's obstacles, Dean Freneau spotted him and leaned graciously out of the carriage. A few people gaped from their windows as the reverend father, whose refinement and elevated seat on his fine carriage made him inaccessible and unapproachable, gave Brandstetter his hand and chatted with him in a friendly manner. Franz was distracted, answering the priest in a confused tone, and was happy when his vehicle set off again.

When Franz Brandstetter stepped over the threshold warped by so many feet under the rounded gateway to his father's farm, a hubbub of voices reached him, which struck him as very odd indeed, given how few people lived under this roof. Perhaps his mother's relatives had come from Waidegg. In the enclosed front porch, the first thing he saw was that the table had been set, but no one was seated at it yet. He looked to see if his mother was in the kitchen, but she wasn't. A stench of burnt cooking came from the stove, which emitted a thin wisp of smoke.

He entered the sitting room and at last found himself facing a whole crowd of people. Jakob Unterberger and his wife Lisa, all the young fellows, Stoffel, Kaspar, the Irgs, Leitgeb, who helped Unterberger in his mayoral office, and maybe ten others were all speaking madly and all at once. Franz caught a few repeated words from the commotion: "... contribution ... payment ... the general ... and Maroni ... Fini ..."

"What on earth is going on? Has there been some sort of an accident?" With these words, young Brandstetter pushed through the group, which was quite large for a sitting room of its size. On the bench built around the square oven, he spied Fini with reddened eyes sitting next to his mother. Standing in the corner next to them was his father, smoking his pipe, attentively following the conversation. Franz tried to find out from those around him what had caused the commotion, but no one answered. They were all declaring their opinions loudly and couldn't imagine that everyone didn't already know about the situation. The student then turned to his mother, and she proved to be the right person to ask. She felt rather uncomfortable in her role as mute listener. The words came bubbling out of her: early in the morning, after he'd left, an unholy racket broke out by the village square. She and Father rushed over. They could already hear the drums. There was a whole crowd of people gathered around a few French soldiers with shouldered weapons standing next to Hauptmann Maroni on horseback, waiting for the general to issue a command. There was a furious uproar that lasted a long time and then finally things went quiet, and a voice proclaimed a decree in convoluted, clever sentences that she didn't understand. The men had a clearer grasp of the situation, of course, but nobody could really make sense of the clever distortion of the truth. One thing was certain: the Hermagorers would have to pay and pay ... A terrible sum had been named. In a word, they would work themselves to death to meet the demand. The reason given was unintelligible—people had only caught a few snippets: Mortal insult ... the whole village must be punished ... General Ruska ...

They shook their heads and stood there for a while, unable to understand. Only gradually did the whole picture get pieced together, and when it did, more than a few veins bulged with outrage. One man vented his anger, a few of the bravest aligned themselves with him, and a perfect popular uprising threatened to ensue. Even Hauptmann Maroni, who saw the world through young, cheerful eyes and was a happy daredevil in battle, began to look uneasy and threw furtive glances at the furious crowd surrounding him and his eight men. He had nothing against these foreign people and was even rather well disposed toward them since life was relatively good here. Nevertheless, the unpleasant situation almost destroyed his goodwill. He weighed the possible responses and decided on a coup de force to surprise the farmers and prevent them from turning violent. Maroni coolly surveyed the situation and signaled his musketeers to prepare, then he burst out of his calm composure with a quick "About face!" so that everyone stepped back in alarm, then he reined in his haste and rode at a walking pace through the living wall, followed by his several soldiers on foot.

As Franz's mother described it all vividly, Fini was listening too, and slowly looked back up.

"... we barely walked in the door when Fini comes to me, completely beside herself, weeping and weeping. We couldn't bear to listen."

And that, then, was how it was.

They were probably the only ones at the Unterbergers' who saw things clearly.

Indeed, they'd been shocked that night when they learned what had happened, namely that Fini had pushed the general off the stairs and that he'd landed in the puddle of muck, provoking laughter among everyone there, including his subordinates. Everyone had secretly been afraid of the consequences, but they perhaps underestimated his response: that Ruska would avenge himself for a personal humiliation so savagely and indiscriminately on the entire local population just to demonstrate to himself and everyone around his absolute authority. Fini especially was utterly devastated, crying nonstop. Not long after this first terrible news, soldiers from Ruska's own guards showed up and started emptying the cellar, armed with a written order from the general, which they showed the innkeeper. They loaded the wine bottles and beer barrels on their cart and didn't leave behind a single liter of brandy. This was a real blow for Jakob Unterberger the innkeeper. His source of income was gone; it had already been thin because of the tight revenue controls, but still, it had been something. The general's notice that he would no longer patronize Unterberger's establishment passed over him as if from a great distance. If only they'd taken away his position as mayor! God knows, in times like these, when the pressures of the office weigh ten times as heavily, he would be happy to see it go.

"That Ruska definitely knows how to knock the stuffing out of people," Unterberger rasped and openly cursed the French, wishing to send them all to the gallows. His wife was now wailing with Fini and he then started cursing her—didn't she have anything better to do—and in the end he unloaded all his bitterness on his wife. More and more people became his targets and finally Lisa grew angry as well. She stood up and wiped her eyes dry: "Pull yourself together. Maybe you think this doesn't affect me as much as you. The whole miserable affair is Fini's fault. She's the one who treated the general so roughly. You can't hold it against him that he liked spending time with her. Didn't I ask you," she turned to the waitress, "to be a bit nicer to him? But you couldn't manage that precisely because it was me who asked you to be nice."

They all looked at each other, but Fini was already up and out the door.

"Well, well," the innkeeper's wife hissed, turning to watch her leave.

What followed was more wild commotion. Unterberger became even coarser than before and shouted that he would never, not ever, allow the girl to be chased from his house by his wife. She better remember that he, Jakob Unterberger, still has something to say. Moreover it's a matter of honor to go after her. Who knows how the poor thing is crucifying herself.

With that, he left too. Lisa followed him in dismay, and all the others followed suit.

Fini had rushed out of the house not knowing where she should go. Lisa's accusation still rang in her ears, she couldn't get it out of her head. She ran as fast as she could, as if someone were chasing her, then she stopped at the Brandstetters' house when it flashed through her mind that the farmer's wife had once given her good, friendly advice, so she looked in the window. She opened her heart to Brandstetter's wife. She didn't care if the farmer listened too because everyone was talking and gossiping about it anyway.

When they came to fetch her, she secretly became a little reconciled. Unterberger and a few others—Kaspar in particular—coaxed her, but Lisa's accusations seemed to have given some the idea that Fini could be their scapegoat, which made things easier for them. A war of words erupted that was far from harmless and full of angry, poisonous looks. Fini, who'd initially hoped things would be resolved, felt her heart sinking once again, and when Franz Brandstetter looked at her after his mother had told him the whole story, he saw that her eyes were swollen and her face was smudged with tears. The cheerful girl from yesterday had changed much for the worse.

The student's eyes burned with agitation. He couldn't believe what he was seeing. He wasn't focusing on the harm the Hermagorers would suffer since he couldn't grasp and feel the full scope of it, either because it didn't affect him directly or else because he'd become estranged from the lives of these people—father and mother, friends and neighbors—from their needs and hardships, without even realizing it. But such a vile mentality, this vindictiveness on the part of the general, whom Franz was seeing as more and more of an enemy, had roused him. He was seized with a rare hatred but could only vaguely imagine how it might be translated into concrete action. The commotion raging around him soon brought him back reality.

Invoking his authority as mayor, Unterberger managed little by little to restore a measure of calm. "So then," he began, "as far as Fini's concerned, I want to say once more—and you can argue as much as you want—it's not the girl's fault. She was wronged. And now she's coming back to the house with me."

He was walking toward her when a brash voice rang out. "But it is her fault. If only she'd been nice to him and not turned him away like that, things would be a lot different for all of us."

Indignant voices rose in support of Fini, but everyone fell silent, and all eyes were on the student who was approaching the man who'd raised the complaint.

"So, because Fini is a decent girl and defends herself, you're going to reproach her? Imagine, if she'd let this gentleman, this fine gentleman General Ruska, have his way, then nothing would have happened to you. You'd be able to joke about the whole thing. You wouldn't have cared what this poor girl went through. As long as you're left in peace. So, why don't you get lost." He yanked the fellow, who had been pushed forward by those around him, and shoved him to the door. "And here's the door, if anyone else has a problem."

Silence fell. Jakob Unterberger was the first to break the tension. He agreed with Franz Brandstetter and made a show of shaking his hand. The others stood like a group of curious schoolchildren, those in the back standing on tiptoe, and, subdued and embarrassed, they voiced their approval.

Fini paid little attention to this important endorsement of her innocence. She sat there, almost as if the whole thing no longer concerned her. Her eyes were fixed on Franz Brandstetter's face. Lisa stepped up to the girl and awkwardly explained that she hadn't meant it that way, of course Fini knew that she'd never have turned her away. Fini nodded and smiled and clasped her hand very tight.

"I'm so happy to hear that."

Moved, Lisa sat down next to her and attributed that happiness to herself and her clever way of changing people's minds. The innkeeper gestured to a few of the heads of the prominent farm households and landlords and asked them to come to the town hall with him. There they could determine how to divide the levies among the various villagers. Soon the Brandstetters were relieved to find themselves alone again, only the innkeeper's wife and Fini were still there, but they were already on their way out. At that moment, the Unterbergers' maidservant stuck her head in the room and when she saw Lisa Unterberger, she moved to the doorstep.

"I'm just wondering if we'll be cooking today. They're already coming in from the fields and complaining," she said.

Lisa exclaimed loudly with a laugh: "Of all things! Now I have to run. Come, Fini!"

"No, Fini is going to stay with us," Brandstetter's wife said as she hurried out of the kitchen. "After that fright, the girl should eat something or at least wait a few hours. My roux was burnt to a crisp but the new one is ready. We'll eat in a moment."

The innkeeper's wife and the girl resisted for a moment, but the farmer's wife was determined.

"But don't be too long!" With that, the maid left Lisa Unterberger and ran to the inn. Fini went into the kitchen with the farmwife to see if she could help. She fumbled around a bit in the unfamiliar kitchen, hurrying because the farmer said he'd soon be back from the town hall. But he was not. The food had long since grown cold, and he still hadn't returned.

Franz Brandstetter stood next to the table in the porch and gazed out the window. He was annoyed that he hadn't left with Kaspar and Hans Irg. Something inside was propelling him to a decision, and he lapsed into thoughts of how terrible it was to stand by helplessly while the enemy committed one outrage after another. The fellows wanted to meet at Unterberger's in the afternoon after quietly ending the workday very early. Franz sensed that he would be initiated into things that were new and strange to him but still compatible with his own plans, and he resented every minute that stood between him and the meeting. He absentmindedly watched as Fini set the pan on the table. Franz's mother decided that they'd waited long enough and told Fini to serve the food. Then she came out to the dining room, but turned around right away because the animals had yet to be fed and they always came first. She was annoyed. This kind of thing simply did not happen, but on a day like this everything fell apart. The food would be cold; she would have to accept it. From the courtyard she called back to them, "Go ahead and start eating without me."

Fini stood there at a loss, her face reddening. She looked at Franz, who made no move to sit down. Then she went up to him with a sudden thought. "Franzl, I'd really like to thank you so much."

He looked at her, surprised. "For what, Fini?"

"Don't pretend. I was just so happy that you stood up for me and put a stop to that man's nonsense."

"Go on, don't mention it."

She didn't know what to say.

"Should we sit down and eat?" she stammered after another pause.

He laughed and immediately obeyed. "I'm very hungry but I don't ever notice until someone points it out."

They dished out their food cheerfully but without speaking. The rough wood table lay between them, long and wide, which kept them from feeling very cozy. At one point, Fini raised her head and looked out the window. "Ah, the dean."

Franz Brandstetter also looked out. Freneau was on his way home, once again in his carriage. The driver sat proudly, and the horses were obviously well groomed.

"I saw him on the way here," the student began, to break the silence, and then continued, showing off a little for the simple girl. "He stopped, of course. We chatted briefly and he was in a very good mood. He's a nice man, Dean Freneau. Not so young anymore and I'm sure you'll all be sad when he passes his position to me—God willing not any time soon. Well, Fini, what will you say when I'm your priest?"

She shook her head, and her face was burning hot.

"No, I can't imagine that. It's not possible. No, no ..." she added.

He was astonished and wondered if she thought he might not be capable. But she probably just didn't understand.

"Say, Franz," Fini began again, "tell me, how are things between you and the reverend dean?"

"God knows he's very fond of me. And he means a lot to me. Imagine how much I am indebted to him! If it weren't for him, my father never would've let his only son leave the farm and have his nephew, you know, young Honditsch who's often here with us, take over the farm. I never would've been as happy as I am now, studying. The reverend dean has done more for me than I could ever thank him for," he told her good-naturedly.

"Yes, you know, I was thinking ... last night, before you all left, I overheard a little of what you were talking about. And you said that you weren't siding with the French. But if Dean Freneau means so much to you, then it can't be true."

"What are you talking about?" Brandstetter said, dropping his spoon.

"The way I see it," she replied, a little afraid, "is soon to become the way everyone else sees it—or even worse—if you're so close to the priest."

"I don't think I understand. Can you explain what you mean?"

"But Franzl, surely you know what kind of person Freneau is."

"I don't know anything at all. Please, if you know something, tell me."

He started shaking, clearly upset, and stood up only to sit down again immediately. The farmwife came in, cleared the dishes, and took the leftover food to warm up in the kitchen. When she was gone, Fini got up and slid onto the bench next to the student.

"You know, I didn't want to alarm you and now I see you really don't have a clue. So it's better if I tell you now than if the others become suspicious and rude and you all end up against each other when you want the same thing in the end ... You probably remember that the dean is from Alsace. And even his name sounds like one of our Frenchmen's here. Well, the year after you left—no, wait, what am I saying, that same fall he went to Alsace. No one thought anything of it. But it turned out that the priest was spying against Austria. And because of that, he traveled to France two more times. Our people can't do anything to him, but it's terrible that someone like this is living right here among us. It certainly makes things easier for the French. Anyway, on his second trip, they caught him and took him to Klagenfurt. A major committee oversaw the investigation. But he must've been very clever because they couldn't prove that he'd been spying. With the French he always acts as if he's neither for or against them, always neutral. But Kaspar knows he'd been meeting with the general in the parish house. Of course, no one heard what they were discussing, but since we found out about the meeting, we've been careful not to say anything in front of the priest. We keep everything secret. I don't understand why, even though the French are everywhere, there are still so many here who make excuses for them. And if the emperor doesn't even object to them, many others won't either. That's the reason we didn't trust you at first. After the way you stood up yesterday and, even when the others were putting on such a show, you kept saying the French were the enemy, then we knew we'd be able to count on you. But believe me, your closeness with Freneau makes everyone suspicious."

Brandstetter's jaw dropped at her words. What he was hearing, what was being revealed to him, was the last thing he would have imagined. It seemed horrible to him. The priest ... Freneau, his teacher and supporter ... no, it was simply inconceivable. At first, he tried to push it aside, laugh it off, and dismiss it as a bad joke—to explain it away as a flimsy idea that couldn't hold. Nevertheless it now seemed perfectly clear, and he was forced to believe it. But this news came so unexpectedly and so quickly that he lost his composure. Fini sat there for a long time, looking at him uneasily.

45

After a while, she began speaking again to break the tension. He thanked her for warning him of the mistake that would've had immeasurable consequences. Still, he was happy when Fini got up and left. She said goodbye to his mother in the kitchen. As she was leaving, she gave a covert glance back at the table.

Franz Brandstetter wondered how he might occupy himself and decided that was best done with work. He split the large logs into smaller pieces, picked out the resinous wood chips and piled them up carefully. He was putting them on the oven for his mother when his father returned. The farmer had never had time to be idle or interrupt his work during the day, but in recent years, he'd been forced to on more than one occasion. He dropped into the chair so heavily it cracked, then lit his pipe. His son looked at him expectantly, but at first he didn't say anything. Only in response to his son's question did he briefly mention the amount he would have to pay. It was a tidy sum; there was nothing more to say. No word could've eased the burden. And so Franz Brandstetter sat with his father in silence, and after a while the latter stood up. He harnessed the horse and led it to the hay barn. He hitched it to the cart with the high wicker sides. The student followed him.

"I'm coming with you today."

The farmer agreed—he had no patience for wasting time. The student didn't mind helping but he was distracted as he worked to fill the wagon with grass clippings and drive it home twice. Then he let the farmgirl take the wagon back to the field and got ready to go the Unterbergers'. He washed and fetched his nicer jacket from the small attic room. But realizing it was still too early, he took a few books and leafed through them. Since they didn't hold his attention he picked up the bible, opened it, and read the words on the page before him. They seemed unimportant. He clapped the book shut and let it fall open again. It was a game he liked to play when he was trying to reach some sort of decision or make a plan. He wasn't at all superstitious or irrational but he would use this game of chance for encouragement or to strengthen his resolve.

"Love your enemies!" jumped out at him in red letters the third time he opened the book. He peered closely at it, to make sure, then angrily tossed it aside. But he immediately picked it up off the bed, where it had sunk into his pillow, and calmly set it on the table. He thought for a while and decided that he could probably love a personal enemy, but not an abstract one, like the French now. They hadn't done anything to him, but he hated them. Maybe it wasn't actual hatred, but it was something very similar. If they'd hurt him, if he'd had to suffer because of them, maybe he could've come to some miraculous love. He thought that he'd never make a good priest—everything inside him was so confused and peculiar: anyone who saw into his soul would condemn him. He wanted to think pious, peaceful thoughts, but he could not escape his ambivalence.

He tidied a few things that were lying around his room and hung his work jacket in the wardrobe. Someone had just entered the house so he and went downstairs. It was his mother. She'd propped her rake in the corner near the door. Hay stems still stuck between its teeth. She had come to fetch the jug of water for the thirsty workers. She asked him if he was planning to go out.

"Yes," he answered curtly.

As he left, strolling slowly along the street, Mateh Banul caught up with him.

"A fine day, today," he smirked.

"Yes, you could say that." The student found the Slovene's manner repulsive.

"Where is it you're headed, if one might inquire?"

"Just to Unterberger's."

"Then we're heading in the same direction. How nice, when it's such a long stretch," he grinned.

They were soon there. Inside all was quiet. Brandstetter was the first to arrive. The peddler saw him glance into the public room.

"Now, hang on. At this hour, we don't get served yet. You're a bit early. Everyone's still out in the field. Come, let's check the kitchen."

From the kitchen came sounds of clattering and banging. Fini, working there alone, greeted them both and asked them to take a seat. As she passed the student, she whispered him that he needed to be patient for a little while longer. Then she brought over a drop of leftover wine and poured twice as much for the student as for Mateh Banul.

"Ah, will you look how a woman pours."

"An old man like you shouldn't drink so much," the waitress retorted.

"Even nicer," the Slovene protested. "Do I look like an old dodderer? I can keep up with any youngster. But I'll be quiet. A girl always gives a dashing young fellow the best wine. Is that true or not? ... He looks good, Franzl does. I'm sure he's caught your eye, but you won't get anywhere with him. The best you can hope for is a visit at confession."

Brandstetter looked at his grotesque face with disgust. Fini brought bread, bacon, and a knife and slammed them on the table in front of the peddler. He just laughed and started paring off thin strips of bacon rind. All the while he talked incessantly as he lifted the bacon to his mouth with shaky fingers.

"... So, and what do you say about Vienna, Franzl? How is it for us out there? Have you ever seen the emperor? What's heard from Napolium? And what do you think? Will things stay this way forever, and will we all become true-blue Frenchmen or not?

He winked at the angry young woman. "What do the girls look like out there? If you take a proper look at ours, the others don't measure up, isn't that right? Look at Fini there. She's grown up fine, with something up front and nicely built in back—cheers you right up."

Mateh Banul looked at Franz Brandstetter's annoyed expression and erupted in another burst of laughter.

The door slammed. Fini had disappeared into the adjacent pantry. The student kept his eyes eagerly fixed on the door, which didn't open right away, but Fini finally came out again. She could feel that Brandstetter really was looking at her for the first time, eyeing her up and down, but shyly. Her cheeks were flushed, and she moved mechanically, as if against her will, aware of being watched. Mateh Banul paused his needling. He'd been deflected. Of course, he couldn't keep his mouth shut completely. There was an agonizing half-hour wait for Brandstetter before the first of the others—Kaspar Unterberger, Irg, and Stoffel Pirker—arrived. Then things sped up. The rest came soon after and the conversation made this last stretch of time pass quickly.

Their group was complete when a band of hot and sweaty Frenchmen came thumping in, led by Hauptmann Maroni, who had been billeted at the inn on Ruska's order that morning along with three other soldiers. From now on, the Unterbergers and Fini would have to sleep in the attic on sacks filled with straw. When everyone was there, the house was bursting at the seams, which was very irritating, as the general had no doubt intended. The soldiers had returned from a march into the Upper Gail Valley and were cursing everything, especially the sun and the dust. Secretly, however, they were cursing the general who had ordered the march. They complained loudly in front of the captain, who was the favorite among their superiors and the only one they liked. He was a fundamentally good sort of person, who didn't begrudge anyone their own pleasure, since he himself had a cheerful disposition and was even-keeled. He loved life with all its trappings, bearing the occasional mishap and deprivation with a smile, because these, too, would pass. He chased every skirt, didn't drink more than the others, and acted in every regard with marvelous abandon. This made Hermagor as pleasant as Paris and Strasbourg because he took what was pleasant and left the rest. He smiled at Fini, who prepared his food, as agreeably as he would at the daintiest, most coquettish of Parisians. While the French soldiers lunged—peacefully, but with a murderous hunger—at their dinner, the young men disappeared up a ladder into the loft above the granary in the barn. They perched on the roof beams in a vague circle and let their feet dangle. They were full of secrecy and stealthiness, which kindled their excitement. Kaspar's description brought the terrible day vividly to life and fanned the flames of their hatred.

Every sound that reached them from the laughing enemies below smoldered in their heads and goaded them on. Their conversation went back and forth, first in a whisper, then louder. Franz Brandstetter, who was also initially enthralled by their clandestine operation, began to sober up. What he heard were simply words, meaningless words that were creating false heat. They were empty and hollow. Their vaunted patriotism and hatred of the enemy was essentially a conceit, an urge for freedom exaggerated by their passion, but they would be unable to explain why they were so worked up. The boys' fathers bore the real burden of quartering the soldiers and the associated unpleasantness and were filled with a justified inner rage, but in God's name it wouldn't have occurred to them to fight a battle with words that would only hamper them further without harming the enemy. They gladly would've fought back had they not immediately realized how pointless it would be. The boys, however, spoke of actions without any real intention of undertaking them. Their ranting was spurred by an illness, albeit a healthy one that afflicts every young person, and eventually leads toward a recovery of some sort. But they did not consider that one day they would think more clearly, more reasonably, and perhaps more soberly. Only the student retreated into his thoughts. His reflections were no more measured than the others', but these repeated words, nothing more than empty words, seemed pointless to him. He had a burning desire to act and would've embarked blindly on even the most foolish plan simply to quench the fire of his inner conflict, to channel it elsewhere and move past it. He kept his opinions and his responses to himself until he was the last to speak. Then with significant effort he began urging them to rise up, to join a conspiracy, and to do it all soon, quickly ... now!

They all cheered. How right he was, this is where to start, ... no, this is!

Franz Brandstetter felt a chill and thought he must look pale since the cold was drawing the blood from his veins. He saw their enthusiasm as a straw fire and, chafing under his own scorn, was the first to suggest that they'd had enough for today. They went on debating. He didn't say another word and was happy when they left the loft as eager as little children.

That evening he drank more than usual. He sat in the kitchen, withdrawn, and watched the peddler who'd spread out his trinkets and baubles and was encouraging Fini and the innkeeper's wife to look and buy. Mateh Banul felt pain in his knee and, exhausted, soon made his bed in the hay. The student remained. At first he'd wanted to make his mother happy and get home on time, but then he pushed this thought aside. The bustling in the kitchen had calmed down and he saw that he was alone with the waitress. He was at the point of leaving, but it suddenly occurred to him it wouldn't be good if it seemed like he was fleeing. He watched Fini, looking at her the way he had that afternoon. He wondered if he found her appealing. He couldn't say for sure. Mostly he saw her back, covered with a gray apron that came all the way down to the floor. He noticed the deep, square neckline. He brushed against her and turned red. Blood shot straight into his head when he looked at her. Fini turned around and cast a questioning glance at him. Thinking they were visibly inflamed, they stared at each other, frightened and ashamed. He turned away and played with the window handle. The flame died down and the only glow in the darkness now came from the stove. Franz felt torn, overcome by a tremor, a mad spinning of his nerves, which made him want to either roar or laugh. A driving rage caused him to clench and open his fists. He felt both rooted in place and pulled into the silent darkness. He wanted to split in two, to push, to plunge, to destroy, all the life in his body convulsing into a wild impulse. The girl stood frozen in expectation and didn't move a muscle. The helplessness that overpowered her kept her from breathing.

Silence fell upon them and Fini recovered more and more. She shrugged her shoulders, turned and groped her way to the stove, and held a fresh splint to the embers. The flaring light blinded her eyes. The student was still standing at the window. Without looking left or right, he slowly left the room.

As he shuffled home along the dark street as if in a daze, he remembered that he hadn't paid.

V

Franz Brandstetter let a few days go by. He didn't go back to the inn and on Sunday he didn't leave the house except for early mass. He read for hours and thought. This yielded both a great deal and nothing. He would picture himself immersed in the events of recent years, which for him were those of his recent days, and then imagine the same events from above, overseeing them critically. His personal experience outweighed everything else, though he was unaware of this—and yet he couldn't shake a feeling of defiance. He wanted to rebel against, as he saw it, the narrow world at home, in which he was trapped by a thousand rules and considerations. He assumed he was completely dependent on the opinion of his fellows precisely because he was one and they were many. He felt like some strange beast that had strayed into a flock of sheep and had started bleating with them just to blend in. He wanted to prove to himself that this wasn't the case, that he was the only one who dared to do something everyone else was against.

In the middle of the week he went to see the priest. He wasn't sure what he was looking for, and he certainly didn't know how he should act. Just as he had earlier been ready to believe all of the rumors, he was now prepared to consider them slander.

Freneau was not in the house. Brandstetter stood there, undecided and annoyed. He had just turned to leave when the priest came over from the church. They greeted each other, the student relieved and happy, the priest with a questioning tone, which he soon expressed directly. He began by saying: "I was wondering why you didn't come for so long. Is there a particular reason or was it just laziness?"

The student was embarrassed, but fortunately Freneau didn't give him a chance to respond, sparing his lying or hypocrisy. At first they'd intended to settle in the study, but then the priest brought the young man into the church. With a mix of joy and pride he told Franz all about the sculptures, pointing out the beautiful carvings—a Saint Joachim and a Saint Anne—and the ornate wrought-iron sconces, describing each of the altars by name. He said that even though this was his home church, Franz surely no longer remembered it and in earlier years the value of the holy objects was the last thing he would've cared about. The student looked around encouraged, but he couldn't suppress the same awful shudder he recently experienced whenever he lingered in a church. He couldn't pay complete attention to what Freneau was saying because he couldn't get the allegations out of his mind, he couldn't stop himself from occasionally studying the priest with a bewildered expression. Apparently he felt the priest could discern his own political stance just by looking at him. After a while, Franz thought he saw Freneau smile to himself, and Franz related this smile to his unspoken doubts about his mentor. Another hour spent together in the parsonage, an old, castle-like building from the end of the fifteenth century, didn't bring Franz any closer to an inner calm. He was unable to focus any more on the priest's words when the latter began recounting his trip to Alsace. Freneau vividly described the magnificent regions he had crossed, losing himself in expansive rapture. The student sensed a reason for the priest's recollections, a mischievous delight behind them. But this wasn't exactly the case, even though the priest was deliberately talking about Alsace. He was waiting for a question from the young man. Franz Brandstetter could no longer contain himself and interjected, "One of my friends has close acquaintances in Alsace and went there himself several times. He completely shares your admiration of the region and the countryside. However, he says that the people, handsome and amiable as they are, have completely forgotten Louis XIV's atrocities and are flirting with the west. Secret intrigues directed against our emperor are not exactly rare, in short, in this region there are as many spies and traitors as people loyal to the emperor. It's disgraceful given that so many of the people there were good Germans."

Freneau smiled. "Franzl, why are you telling this to me? Don't you know that Alsace is my homeland? Don't get worked up, it's nothing serious. I'm not insulted but I do want to say something about this to you. You claim that everything there is still German. My dear boy, just look at my name. In Klagenfurt they always write 'Freno.' Maybe they think it looks more in keeping with this nation. Maybe, I don't know. I refuse to believe that you, too, are worried about such quibbles when it's clear you can't stop thinking about this. But many things can be overcome."

The student was speechless at how cleverly the priest had extricated himself. He must know what was being said about him! Franz didn't have the courage to face him and ask bluntly—his respect for the priest was an even greater obstacle. He tried to tame the anger that seized him when he looked into Freneau's twinkling eyes. The priest recognized the young man's emotions and responded with kindness. "Franz, you expected a different answer. Is that right?"

The student remained silent, revealing what was already clear.

"You think," the reverend priest continued, "that I would say in all conscience that this isn't the truth of the matter, or that being chastened I would admit or confirm it, or that I would defend myself with endless explanations. Franzl, I did none of these during the trial in Klagenfurt and I won't with you today either … Why? Look, should I offer something to people when they enjoy guessing so much? Believe me, they prefer uncertainty about my existence than any loud proclamation of truth. I let others have their opinions. If today someone thinks I'm capable of treason, then he will assume I am. An acquittal won't change his ability to discern the truth, and if the opposite is the case, then my previous statement would be different. There's also something to be said for letting the opinion of the court speak for itself."

"Father, didn't you present anything in your defense in Klagenfurt?" Brandstetter asked in agitated disbelief.

That Franz was clearly shocked by such an extravagant stance, and that it probably struck him as nothing more than a lie both cheered and saddened Freneau.

"Certainly not," Freneau looked down, "I did not offer, confirm, or refute a single word. I left it up to the wisdom and intuition of those presiding. I was acquitted for lack of evidence. Naturally, from a certain standpoint—in this case an Austrian one—this result is not a verdict on my guilt or innocence. I view the judgment issued by the committee the way I would a statement made by an individual, as a sign of innate ability."

No further explanation followed, and the student was forced to draw his own conclusions from these idiosyncratic views.

Much later, he found himself in the meadows that flank the Gössering riverbed. The earth brought him the damp breath of the river and quickened his mind. He understood Freneau's behavior intellectually but could not make sense of it with his heart. Once again, he felt so confused and paralyzed by recent events that he forced himself to redirect his thoughts. That was good. He closed his eyes and slowly concentrated on one number after another. It was a childish remedy, the type of habit that he turned to whenever he wanted to calm down. He opened his eyes and gazed into the delicate sea of clouds in the summer sky. In such moments he wished that he could paint, that he could depict with all the power of his physical senses the spirituality—or better, the sobriety—of the scene that words failed to convey. Released from all confining surroundings, he pondered this deficiency of existence, which, to make matters worse, gives immortality to words and impermanence to physical form. Then he pressed his hands to his face and laughed heartily, yet his laughter was tinged with grief because he was aware of his many often contradictory wishes and opinions swirling in helpless confusion and striving in vain to find unity and a fixed center. His emotions were as volatile as his inclinations. Heading toward the road he felt a strangely melancholic sense of homeland, of belonging to this place—and this feeling was somehow different from when he was abroad. He wanted to rejoice, but could only weep, deadened by something he didn't recognize.

A sharp wind blew from the south, carrying the sand of the Gail in its mouth, which gusted into people's eyes, making them red and sore. It shook the forests until the trunks whirled helplessly and the leaves trembled and wailed. It whipped up a roar. Each step was a struggle, the body bent forward to cut the air more easily. Franz Brandstetter felt like he was being kicked and in his current mood, he was doubly aware of the harshness of nature, which seemed to epitomize his fate. He felt weak in the face of nature and panted. He wanted to be able to grow from this, but his efforts were pitiful. The Gail River carries sharp sand, just like life. It flows calmly, it flows wildly. Here the water creeps leadenly as if resting or before its final rest, while a rough stone might lie on the bed causing the water to swirl and foam as it scrambles over. The water catches the thin-hulled boat and pulls it under. There are thousands of such maelstroms in the river and beyond it, where they are no less dangerous. But it's certainly the case that after such struggles—which are never fought to the bitter end—one must return, still hot and churned up from the far side of thought, one must return to the here and now.

Such was the state of the student's mind when he arrived home. The wind hadn't eased the heat from the day, yet he felt chilled, and so he enjoyed the warmth of fire. His mother poured cornmeal from the fine burlap sack into the water and immediately stirred the steaming, thickening mass. The vapor, filled with the delicious flavor, spread around the room and prodded all the hungry stomachs.

The farmer sat with the older Irg, and Franz listened to them attentively. They were talking about how they'd manage the levies.

"Maybe you know how to raise the money?" his father jeered.

"As little as you."

"They won't spare you. You can't be considered poor any more than I can. What will you do?"

"Maybe I'll borrow it."

"Who from? You think creditors grow like the leaves on the trees?"

"Doesn't have to be someone in Hermagor. I think I'll look around in Sankt Stefan or in Vellach. A few of my father's relatives live there."

"Nice if it works out for you. But introduce me to your relatives. I'm sure they'll give us a loan without making us put up any reasonable collateral. We can sit here until Judgment Day, until our shirts disintegrate and fall off."

"You're right. But tell me a better idea if you've got one."

Brandstetter said nothing. He knocked his pipe clean. His wife stepped between the two men with the large pan, the milk jug, and the bowls, and ladled out the liquid. The bent and battered tin spoons slowly sprinkled the crumbly corn into the milk until it formed a porridge, then moved quickly up to the eager mouths to ease the hunger.

The student ate and scraped the last bits from his bowl, wiped his lips with the back of his hand, and watched the two old men with interest.

"Wouldn't it," he picked up the men's thread from earlier, "wouldn't it be best if you sold a few fields? Each of you could sell one to people in Vellach or Watschig. You'll never come up with the money any other way."

The two farmers gaped at him. Brandstetter burst into laughter. He shook his head and couldn't get enough. "Hah. You hear that?" he nudged his neighbor. "What an idea. This is what you get when you let the boys study. Don't let the same thing happen to you." The suggestion had struck him as sheer madness.

Franz was not insulted. He carefully reviewed the situation but couldn't come up with another solution. His earlier feeling of indifference threatened to reappear. The two men resumed their conversation.

"It's impossible, of course," Irg said, in confirmation.

"That's what I say. Those who know nothing about it don't understand a thing. You don't just decide to sell a field at the drop of a hat, not around here."

"It's the Frenchman's fault, that dog," Brandstetter grumbled again.

"Complaining doesn't help anyone. There's been enough of that already!"

"Don't be stupid. If you don't have any idea where to start, then keep your mouth shut."

"Then you keep yours shut, too."

"I'll complain as much as I want."

"You've done your fair share already."

"No more than you."

They went on calmly needling each other. The student said a brief good night to the men and his mother and went upstairs to bed.

Later the two old men become increasingly monosyllabic and when Irg was about to leave he said thoughtfully, "When I think about what Franzl said ... I'm not so sure it was stupid after all. In a few years, we could buy back the fields. What do you think, should I tell Unterberger?" Brandstetter half admitted that he was coming around to the idea, too.

"If you think so," he said. The two men couldn't part so quickly, since it was only at this point that they'd begun to have a fruitful discussion. They got up and walked around the courtyard. The farmwife had long turned in when her husband finally crept into bed next to her.

At noon the next day, the sun was shining very brightly, but homely, gray wisps of clouds came floating over Trogkofel Mountain. They were moving fast, circling the peak, and their dance heralded a coming storm. The air was so charged with heat that some claimed you could strike sparks from it.

A farmer's instinctual wisdom about the weather was alien to Franz Brandstetter, but even he sensed that the heat was threatening to turn into rain or a storm. He'd worn his sleeves rolled up since morning and couldn't summon the energy to join in the work. He pretended to focus on his own studies, even though he was bothered whenever his parents shook their heads over his shirking. He crept up the hanging ladder with a book and squeezed in among the attic rafters. It was dusty and stifling up there. He was free from the black flies and horse flies, but the whirring motes stung his nose and breathing became difficult. The student soon snapped his book shut, perched closer to the roof, and peered down through a missing shingle. The street was empty. Only a filthy dog roamed around, sniffing in every corner and lifting its leg. Even the chickens must've fled to the cooler gardens and fields.

A small person was marching toward the farm from the direction of Vellach. As the figure drew closer, it was clear that this was a small, sturdy boy carrying a knotted cloth. He kept close to the walls, sometimes scraping against them, so that his tunic turned white and stone-gray and nearly tore. When he came close to the Brandstetter's farm, he crossed the street and Franz lost sight of him.

The sound of the door and footsteps in the house caught his attention and he climbed downstairs.

He heard his mother's loud, chatty voice, which was answered by a clear, young one. It's the boy, Franz thought, but he wasn't sure who this was.

He stepped into the kitchen, and everyone fell silent.

"Well," the farmwife cried, "it's Franzl—Irgl boy, give him your hand!"

"Look at that," Franz said with a laugh, "Irgl, our little farmer. So how do you like the Brandstetter farm?"

"Very much," Irgl stuttered in reply. He stared wide-eyed at Franz—this young man, who lived in Vienna, in the city where the emperor lived, and studied theology. He'd become such a gentleman, even if he was wearing shabby work clothes. Still, you only had to look him in the eye.

Franz's mother brought some bacon and bread, and milk to quench his thirst. Vellach isn't too far away, but this heat can make a man weak. She first carved the three crosses into the fresh loaf of bread, then cut three finger-thick slices off.

"Boy, has the cat got your tongue?" she cried. Irgl looked past the student with a shy smile. Then he unpacked his bundle.

"Mother sent cheese because it hasn't been easy for you here."

"But, but ..." Franz saw his mother protesting. "You should have it yourself since you're a growing boy."

In the end, she accepted the cheese. It was true that the surrounding villages had it better. Recently, the French had been requisitioning the entire yield of the Hermagor farms, along with their penalty fine.

Franz Brandstetter took a close look at Georg Wernitznig, the boy from Honditsch. So this was the future owner of the Brandstetter farm. This solid, healthy face over which a dark shock of hair towered like defiance incarnate. A furtive examination of the boy didn't reveal a single family resemblance that stirred Franz's feelings. The boy was an outsider. Franz felt a certain bitterness as he looked around the room and through the open door to the front porch, where the rakes and scythes stood. Not one of them felt comfortable in his hands, but they were his father's tools, it was his father's house. He was painfully aware that for the time being it was still his house, but once young Honditsch came of age, it would belong to someone else, Franz's footsteps would merely be tolerated, he would be cast out. Then he would belong in the parish house.

The parish house had dignified gray walls but Franz hated gray masonry. He preferred light or bare, unpainted stonework, and yet his only aspiration was to celebrate the elation of his soul within such quiet walls. Yes, everything was as he had wished. How could Franz be angry with his father when everything had been his wish and his wish alone. The house would become part of the Honditsch farm because for once his own will had been stronger than his father's.

His thoughts grew ever more heated. He reflected that he could hardly envy the child's worldly goods that he'd helped him acquire, and he tried to stay calm. Franz noticed that the boy hadn't said a word in his presence, he shifted from one bare foot to the other out of embarrassment. Franz had correctly guessed that he was causing the boy's shyness, so in the end he stood up. He wanted to say something, to defend himself and his decisions, but instead he brushed his fingers over the loaf of bread, then turned abruptly, and left the room. The farmwife watched him, astonished.

"What a lunatic!" she laughed, turning to the startled boy. "So what does your mother think of the crazy story—you know what I mean, because of the new payments we have to make..." she asked and continued chatting...

Franz Brandstetter paced aimlessly between the barn and the house. The air trembled and a soft rumbling came from the Carnic Alps. He wasn't paying attention to anything. He glanced in the woodshed, but there was already enough kindling in it. The cows lay in the stall, chewing their cud, restlessly moving their heads and clumsily swinging their tails. Soon the first cow stood up and one by one the rest followed. A pile of cut grass from the morning stood by the door. Franz threw a bunch to each animal: it wouldn't hurt, he thought, for them to eat off their schedule. He held his palm out to the horse, and it opened its mouth. He stroked it and pressed his head against its neck, feeling the beat of its warm blood.

As a result, he missed the first flash of lightning. Suddenly his body was shaken by the powerful booming and rumbling of the thunder. The animals stamped about fretfully, spreading their agitation to him. He didn't want to be caught off guard in the half darkness of the stall, so he stood on the doorstep and looked up toward the sky. Overcoming his initial inhibitions, he enjoyed the blazing spectacle of colors and was spellbound as he eagerly awaited the next display.

His mother appeared in the doorway of the house. "Franzl... Ah, there you are. Come in before the storm starts," she shouted into the wind that swirled up the dust.

The first drops fell; they were so big that you could almost hear each one hitting the ground. The droplets came down in bunches, settling the clouds of dust. Soon there was only a pattering noise, and the sky that had blazed so colorfully and had been filled with clouds, now sank to the earth, opaque and gray. It poured down in streams. Lightening flashed ever farther off, leaving only the rain.

The farmer rushed around the corner of the house. He hurried in from the street and stopped, panting, under the eaves. He saw his son and nodded to him. Franz stood undecided, then quickly bounded over to his father's side. He smoothed his hair and brushed off the back of his shirt. The rainwater from that brief moment was trickling down his spine.

"Well, what's new? What has our Bürgermeister decided?" he asked mockingly.

The older Brandstetter scraped the stone with his foot.

"Hmm, you haven't heard, but last night Irg and I talked things over some more."

"Talked what things over?"

"That maybe we'll have to sell a few fields."

"And?"

"Today we suggested it to Unterberger."

"That's impossible."

"Why not? He agreed."

In the cold light of day, the actual implementation of this struck Franz as inconceivable. "But that's madness!" he cried. His father shot him a look.

"There's no other way. And what does it matter to you? You won't own the farm in any case. Irgl will always have enough because he has the Vellach property, too."

Franz Brandstetter lowered his head. His ardor collapsed. The farm was none of his business. He'd wanted it this way. And selling the fields and pastures had been his advice only yesterday. It was as if his every word, his every movement was coming back to mock him.

"Who will have to sell?" he asked indifferently.

His father named the local farmers who were better off. The

meadows along the road from Vellach would be sold to farmers in Obervellach. They still had money, they were the lucky ones who'd been less bothered by the French.

Unterberger had immediately called on Hauptmann Maroni at headquarters to obtain selling rights and with a leaden voice he stated the reason, which of course the soldier must've already known. The clerk had laughed. Maroni remained gracious and took care of the matter right away. He ran into Relioz at Ruska's, where the two were playing cards, which had put the general in a very cheerful mood. Maroni received Ruska's authorization, which circumvented the only possible obstacle to the sale.

Such courtesy caught Unterberger off guard, and so he continued to direct his anger at the young officer.

Franz Brandstetter didn't know how to respond to his father's account.

"Who on earth is that?" The old man's question, asked in a low voice, caught Franz's attention. He glanced over at the hay barn. A woman came rushing over, as if running for her life. She stopped to catch her breath, then ran toward the house, without noticing the men.

"It's the Mölzer woman," the student said, quickly recognizing her. He watched, tense and uncomfortable.

"What's the matter?" the farmer asked when she ran a few steps past him, keeping her head down. Vaba hadn't stopped by the Brandstetter farm in years. She'd been a maidservant there, but had inconspicuously steered clear of the household since she left. The farmer was surprised. The woman started when she heard his voice and stood stock-still in the rain with her eyes closed.

At that moment, the farmer's wife had heard the men talking and she opened the door to call them in. The first thing she saw was Vaba Mölzer. She was struck dumb. Then she reflexively placed her hand on her hip. "Well ..." she groaned, "well ..."

Then she raised her voice. "How can such a slut come back to our farm? Get out of here, I'm telling you, go ... or ..."

The man watched mutely, and the son raised his hand, appalled. "But mother ..."

Brandstetter's wife looked at her son: what a poor boy he was. She was offended that he'd objected to her anger and was sorry that she'd snapped at the woman. Maybe Franz had once been fond of Vaba and maybe her boy, who she was so proud of, had gained something thanks to the girl. She found a life of abstinence inconceivable.

"Well, in God's name, come over here until it stops pouring. Mölzer, we can't keep avoiding each other our entire lives out of spite ... I was just thinking that."

Her family looked at her and couldn't believe their ears.

"Don't stand and stare. All of you, come into the kitchen," she urged them again.

"Fine," was all the farmer said. It had nothing to do with him. It was women's business. They would need to figure out how to get along.

Vaba quietly followed the others into the house and stood, leaning against the wall of the enclosed porch. The student was amazed that she did so, after having been insulted. Very few words were exchanged between the raindrops that tapped ceaselessly on the roof. Even the farmwife was at a loss. The men repeatedly checked the weather, and soon the farmer was gone. He wanted to repair the rake that kept slipping from its wooden handle and to double-check the other tools and baskets. The first potatoes were ready to be dug. Irgl nibbled slowly at his bread and bacon, unable to swallow much of it. Franz had gone back to stand by the door.

The rain let up and the sky brightened over the mountains. The clouds dispersed and drifted away. The ground couldn't absorb all of the rain from the sudden deluge and the water stood in puddles or streamed away. The rain hadn't lasted long. For the farmers it was too little after the long drought but they were happy that at least the ground was wet.

Vaba got ready to leave.

"Maybe in the evening you could stop by," the farmwife suggested, to tighten the bond. "You always made such pretty patterns. And I could use one on the tablecloth."

It was no time for needlework or sewing or spinning, but nothing better had occurred to her in that moment. Vaba Mölzer didn't look surprised. She nodded and left with a mumbled goodbye.

In the evening she actually came. The farmwife was milking the cow with the Windish maid. She let the girl finish by herself and went with Vaba into the house. She didn't have any fabric suitable for a tablecloth. She searched the house, opening drawers and chests.

"I simply must have mislaid it," she said, shaking her head. "There's no rush and it's nicer to do needlework in the winter. I'll just have you do it then … but, but you don't need to go now. First, I have to cook supper for all the farmhands, you should stay. It was me who asked you to come."

Vaba didn't talk much right away. She was a peculiar and reticent person.

When it was time to eat, the farmer came in, lit his pipe at the fire, and interrupted the women's conversation. "Was someone chasing you this afternoon?" he asked. His wife turned to look at him. She was tempted to laugh. Vaba opened her eyes slightly, looked at him in surprise, and shrugged.

She wasn't an easy person to figure out.

"Do you still have that one cow?" the farmwife asked.

"Yes," she replied. "But I'll have to slaughter it soon."

"What for?"

"I'm out of feed."

"Oh dear," Brandstetter's wife sighed, "it's the same for all of us. You probably heard that we had to sell the better pastures."

Vaba grimaced. What a cruel joke that the Brandstetters had too little hay and feed. Even with less, they would still have enough.

"How many chickens do you have?" The woman's curiosity was relentless.

"Four."

"So you have enough grain? ... The damned animals eat half our crop. Kondaf will surely have some to spare for you."

"Not nearly enough," she admitted.

The student entered just as she was saying these words. She fell silent and closed her eyes. The meal continued in silence. Franz raised his head briefly. "When did the boy leave?"

"Irgl? Oh, about two hours ago. He couldn't say goodbye to you because you'd gone out," his mother replied.

"It makes no difference," he muttered, trying to put an end to the topic.

But she kept talking. "Franzl, are you all right? He often looks like that, right? I just mean that you should give the books a rest for once. And you don't have to work in the fields. Just take it easy and sit with the other boys in the evening. People on holiday should look happy."

"That's his business," old Brandstetter raised his head and said, "He certainly knows if he's sick or not."

Franz looked at him in disbelief. His father's words did him more good than his mother's and he began to wonder what was wrong with him. Maybe it was all of the idleness. But he had a feeling it was more than that.

"You," Brandstetter ordered his wife once he'd finished and stretched his legs out before him. "Give Vaba a little chicken feed. We won't miss it."

"My word, do we have any left?" she lamented.

"There's a bag of wheat and barley hanging up in the barn. Give her some of that."

"I don't know where it is, and I certainly won't find it in the dark."

"Then Franzl can go look. He saw it today."

The student nodded and left. When he reached the loft, his mother's voice called after him, "Wait, you need a little sack!"

He bent forward and waited.

It was late but still twilight. Close as night was, complete darkness had not yet fallen. The earth had dried again; the air was clear, warm, and washed clean.

The dark figure of a woman crossed the courtyard. It was Vaba. He wanted to go down to get the sack from her, but he kept climbing, with a different intent. He groped toward the grain, which was stored in the other half of the barn. The side near the door was for straw, and it was half-full of hay.

The woman climbed up after him and stopped on the other side. Her clothes looked black in the gray shadows. Franz Brandstetter thought she would follow him and he turned to face her. But she didn't move. He moved toward her, a few hesitant steps, then a few more. Straw was once again under his feet. Its crackling excited him. He stood in front of the woman and saw the pale sack slip from her fingers. He sensed her oddly closed eyes. She opened them and he felt their dark glowing ardor. Her hand pulled the neckerchief from her throat. It fell to the floor and her fingers reached up again to the top button of her dress.

He was in a fever. He was ready to grab her. Her throat was blazing white.

Loud footsteps startled them. The woman clenched the top button in her fist.

"I'll have to look for it myself. You'll never find it in the dark." It was the farmer. He climbed the last few steps and peered around sharply. The boards creaked as he crossed the floor.

"Give me the sack!" he called from the granary. Vaba bent down, picked up the sack and the cloth, and walked slowly toward the farmer.

Franz Brandstetter didn't move a muscle. He heard the rustle of the grains that felt as if they were spilling down his back. Without a word, the three climbed back down, the student last.

VI

The next day dawned, bringing incredible changes and a wave of new events. Tired and gloomy, Franz Brandstetter was slipping into his clothes when he heard Kaspar Unterberger's voice trumpeting through the house's late morning silence. Annoyed, the student hurried to the intruder.

"Finally, there you are," the innkeeper's son greeted him with lively eyes. "Come on, let's go, don't waste time with questions," he commanded, pulling the hungry boy after him. The inn seemed deserted, and it was half-empty since the French had left and taken their horses, as Hauptmann Maroni had informed Fini. The general had ordered them on another march in the Upper Gail Valley.

Like so often, Franz Brandstetter followed the younger Unterberger into the back room and saw all the fellows from Hermagor. This time he spotted a stranger in their midst. No longer young, he was short and slender with dark eyes and a pointed nose. He spoke in a clear voice and broke off when the two entered.

"Hello Leiterer," Kaspar called, "here we have the last of ours. You know, the student. Now tell us one more time what's going on! Tony Leiterer is from Lesach Valley, from Maria Luggau," he added for Franz's benefit.

"Fine, I'll say it for the third time," the stranger laughed. "We, the Lesachers and some of the Tyroleans have been in contact with Austrian military units for a long time now. Obristleutnant de Mumb, maybe you've heard his name, is planning our liberation—surely there's secret permission from above against the French and their allies. As you can imagine, we're all very eager to do this and it's a point of honor that we, all of us from the Gail Valley, are ready and willing. It would be an utter disgrace if we let the Viennese do all of the heavy lifting while we sit idly by. We just assured de Mumb that we can send him at least two hundred men from these parts. And our people have sent me to organize. I've been on the road for three days, moving from one place to the next. Always traveling on back roads at night and the main thing is to keep from falling into the hands of any guards. Early this morning, everything almost went awry. I didn't think there'd be any danger on an empty secluded road, but then an entire brigade of those French devils were advancing upon me. I'm exaggerating a little but, you know, it was the ones who've been tormenting you here in Hermagor. Thank God I was able to slip away in time. So now I'm here and I'm asking for the third and final time if you want to join us."

"Yes … Yes … Of course we do!" voices bellowed from all sides.

"Quiet!" the Lesacher thundered over them. "That's the answer I was hoping for. Sit down so we can talk quietly. First of all, you have to be ready in a few days. Are you up for it?"

This, too, was followed by enthusiastic agreement. Franz Brandstetter was reeling. What did they want from him? What was he doing among these men of war? … "You should use your swords to preach peace," echoed inside him a thousand times. But he was already seized by the will to action and felt excited. And yet it was madness even to suggest he might join them—much less to actually fight alongside them. In October he was supposed to be back in Vienna. He would again attend courses and the revelations of theology would again take hold of his mind and soul, and his vacation would feel like a distant dream.

And now he was tempted by something uncertain, something he'd quietly longed for. It would be liberating to toss everything aside, to throw away his entire predetermined future, in which the path was already clearly laid, to leave it all behind and escape the unhealthy arousal, the thoughts that whirred back and forth in his mind, that stung and tormented him, that blithely poured poison into every cell of his brain. To escape it all and find unity, to attain peace: this was a glorious madness. He would set out now, fighting for his native soil, for his homeland! The madness was intoxicating, it stripped away all earthbound impediments. There were the fields and meadows of his father's farm, his house, the cool porch, the kitchen with the large oven and the crucifix in the corner and not the cold, gray parish house on the market square.

"So then, you all are certain. And what about Brandstetter? What do you say?" Tony Leiterer turned to the dismayed Franz.

The words hit the student hard and he was suddenly horrified. What would Freneau say? But no, he wasn't the one deciding. Even more, what would his father say? Little more than "that's his business." Because you can set your mind to one thing, but you rarely have a chance to turn back. He couldn't stand before his father and say, "I think I've changed my mind again. I'd rather set out with the others and then come home and take up on the farm. I never concerned myself with it and it could've gone downhill in the meantime, but now I'm here and I want to take over the farm because that's the path I prefer." He was certainly exaggerating, but this was essentially what he would need to say.

With a half smile on his lips, he looked at each of his fellows in turn. He saw their inquisitive faces. Not one of them could understand what he was going through and if he said "no" after they'd all made up their minds they would despise him, cast him out, and this first night's test would be nothing compared to what would await him later. He thought that if he could overcome his shame and embarrassment, it would be easier for him to say no. But now it was all the same. Everything had already been decided, and it was ridiculous to think he had any personal freedom of action. He smiled and his hands hurt as if he'd burned himself.

"I'm going with you. That goes without saying!"

The general enthusiasm rose again. Kaspar Unterberger was

the only person there who had some idea of his difficulties. "Well, what will you tell them at home later? And don't you have to go back to Vienna?"

Franz Brandstetter trembled. "But it's simple. I won't tell my parents where I'm going. Otherwise, they wouldn't let me leave. Besides, you'll all have to do the same. And by October, we'll have thrown the French out. I'll get to Vienna when I'm supposed to and pretend like nothing had happened. What happens to me at home is nobody's business and no one will find out about my stint as a soldier. Obristleutnant de Mumb will surely take me on with no other questions and be happy that he has enough men."

He said this without thinking, at first simply responding to his friend's question, but when he said these last words he felt relieved.

Yes, that's how he'd do it! What had occurred to him, on the spot, without thinking, would be his way out. It could all be over by October, and he could go back to university in Vienna. There was no need to completely change course. Eluding his parents with some pretext wouldn't be so hard, or even better: they would eventually come to terms with his running off, and then they would rejoice to have him back in one piece. More and more he was able to repress the shame that had impeded his thinking ...

"That's the right answer!" Leiterer shouted over Franz's deliberations. "Come autumn we'll all be done fighting and there won't be any more Frenchies here, even if the emperor offers Napoleon his friendship ten times over."

He was again hailed with cheers, and hands reached out to the student in agreement.

An hour of heated debate, clouds of billowing smoke, and drinks conjured out of nothing were passed around on that bright morning. The house staff and the waitress had been banished from the room, so the gathering bore all the signs of a conspiracy. Yet the result was that, with the exception of Franz Brandstetter, the fellows decided to let their parents in on their scheme, along with anyone else they could trust, in order to facilitate their plans and not leave their families distressed by unnecessary fears. Promises of freedom and a better future would dispel their misgivings. The following night—they wouldn't be ready to set off any sooner—would provide cover for their movements, and they would travel over the Kreuzberg Pass into the free Drava Valley. They left the rest to fate or, better, to the will of Obristleutnant de Mumb.

By evening, the young men's plans were an open secret. Everyone was moved and alarmed but ultimately convinced by the necessity of their plan.

Before Franz Brandstetter left his house for the inn that evening, his mother put one hand on her hip and wiped her eyes with the other: "You know, Franzl, today, for the first time, I'm truly happy that you're studying and that you don't have to leave like the others."

The student quickly bent over and grabbed the cat that was playing at his feet. His mother's gruffness had often hurt him and left him feeling cold and distant toward her, but today, when he was only afraid of lying to his father, he felt small and mean next to her artless candor. With his head lowered, he kept ruffling the cat's warm fur and was glad when he was soon able to leave and walk up the street.

He saw the parish house and recalled his earlier meeting with the priest as he was heading home at midday. The encounter had been rather inconsequential. But he couldn't get the dean's look of superiority out of his mind. Freneau's expression when they parted had seemed both pitying and knowing. He couldn't keep from seeing Freneau as a peculiar and rare character who preferred to appear aloof to his parishioners and enigmatic to his equals or at least to those who were close to him. Meanwhile his outward bearing often displayed a childishness and a narrowness of vision. Franz Brandstetter needed to stop thinking about Freneau so that he wouldn't continue to worry.

He stood by the inn's entrance and glanced into the kitchen. The innkeeper, his wife, and Kaspar were inside. In the corner by the washtub for the glasses, Hauptmann Maroni was bantering with Fini.

Kaspar called Franz in. He gave Fini a covert nod and she soon disappeared with the officer, taking him first into the stall and then back into the inn's public room. Maroni made a joke of it and let the pretty girl lead him by the nose. It was his habit to let women have their way, while he bided his time.

Franz Brandstetter had told the Unterbergers all about his delicate situation, and they now spoke to him in quiet, urgent tones. From the public room they could hear the noise of the carousing soldiers. Their secrecy was hardly necessary since the French barely understood a word of the local language, unlike the inhabitants who, over three years of occupation, had learned a little bit of French, whether they liked it or not.

Lisa went straight into practical matters, saying she would prepare him some food for the journey and would otherwise look after his things. He thanked her and Unterberger nodded, satisfied with the course of events. Kaspar would go to Irg's that night and stay until they set off, since their house was full of French soldiers who could easily notice their departure. The student would have to spend the night at home as usual to keep up appearances.

In the back room, Brandstetter and the innkeeper's son joined the others. There was a lot of grinning and winking. They talked of trivial things and their eyes shone with excitement and the thrill of the unknown. They thought of themselves as great stage actors and were enjoying their—in their view—brilliant role-playing. They intended to sit together like they usually did so they wouldn't attract attention. They didn't think the French would be completely oblivious to them, but they realized their own responses were gradually becoming dumber and more distracted. Others, especially the student, seemed utterly bored. Franz Brandstetter's drowsiness came less from a healthy need for sleep than from a melancholy mood on his second to last evening home. The next evening could hardly count since it was overshadowed by their impending flight.

The student smiled when he realized the sheer foolishness of their furtiveness and discretion. Tomorrow evening, in the decisive moment before the act, who would manage to sit here in the back room and keep up appearances? Still, he said nothing against this useless playacting. Somehow it was supposed to help with their morale and excitement.

There was nothing to drink. A few of them cast begging looks at the waitress. Fini laughed and brought them a jug of water. This cheered them up slightly. Brandstetter noticed that she wouldn't meet his eyes, lowering her gaze at him as if out of shyness. He was aware that lately he'd been thinking about her more and more, and that some of her movements and glances, which he'd hardly noticed before, now seemed so vivacious. He was convinced that her conduct toward him showed some measure of devotion, and he'd been thinking of her with more warmth, especially in those days when he had been so withdrawn. This thought awoke the memory of the previous night. He pictured Vaba standing in front of him. Like an animal, he thought. But he would've followed through, he was certain, because he had desired the thrill of it and he wanted that thrill since he was still plagued by yesterday's doubts and wanted to stifle them. But he was also relieved that it hadn't come to that.

He grew more downcast. How far he'd come in just a few days. The past years had brought him the purest, most beautiful thoughts. But he hadn't noticed how flimsily constructed they were, since he was able to demolish then in an instant.

Fini finally stole a glance at him. He looked into her kind eyes and quickly turned away.

The soldiers were tired and left the inn much earlier than usual. The waitress started cleaning up. The boys wanted to leave too but a few of them hounded young Unterberger to find something to drink. He finally gave in. Franz Brandstetter leaned against the doorframe and watched Fini. She pretended not to notice and began setting the chairs and benches on the tables. He came over and gave her a hand. She nodded with a faint smile but didn't look up. Then she got the broom and swept, leaving him alone with his thoughts. Together, they put the furniture back on the floor.

One-eyed Irg watched them and laughed. One of the boys went to look for Kaspar, who was taking forever and finally returned with him.

"Sorry boys. All gone. There's a hole in the barrel," he laughed.

They swore cheerfully and stumbled off their chairs. Stoffel Pirker stretched his arms and yawned. "Let's go ... Children, this is our last night at home. This time tomorrow, we're off."

"Well then, off to bed," the innkeeper's son cheered, urging them out the door.

"But not alone," one of them quipped.

At the last moment, the student had lost sight of Fini. He would've liked to say good night to her, so he waited in the courtyard after the others had left. He couldn't really go back in, much as he wanted to, so he finally decided to leave after all. They ran into each other at the corner.

"Don't be frightened. It's me, Fini," she said quickly. He was startled.

"What are you doing out here? Are you waiting for someone?"

"Maybe," she shrugged. They walked together, without a second thought.

"For who?" he laughed.

"He'd have to ask," she mocked him.

He was no longer listening to her, and his mind wandered. "Now it's completely dark. Tomorrow at this time, tomorrow at this time!" He quickly turned toward her. Was she crying? He put his arm around her as they walked.

"Fini ..."

"You ..."

"Fini, are you sad that I'm leaving?"

She did not answer. But she suddenly stopped and turned to face him. He pulled her closer, and they kissed and kissed.

"Fini ...?"

She sighed and clung to him.

"You like me that much?"

"More than I can say."

He couldn't bear to let go of her. "And tomorrow I have to leave."

"And we had to save everything for the last day," she lamented. He tried to console her without saying a word.

Shyly, she pulled away. "Look where we are already."

"In the dark and that's lovely," he joked.

"I believe those are the Irgs' fields and that's the forest behind them."

Trembling, she pushed him away.

"Tomorrow I have to leave," he pleaded and felt her weakness.

"You …" He picked her up with a strange strength. The hay lay in thick piles. The strong, spicy smell numbed and stifled all resistance.

The following night was just as dark and warm. The small band walked quietly and were more at ease as they moved further away from town. They skirted Podlanig's buildings, too, even though they presented no danger. The man from Lesach walked in front with the innkeeper's son. Franz Brandstetter was some distance behind them, alone. In one hand he held Fini's gift, which she'd brought to him that afternoon. It was good to know he was cared for.

Now and then a word interrupted the monotony of their steps. But that was rare. The hours raced ahead as they marched along. The night was unusually dark, and that reinforced their silence.

The dawn of the new morning brought a sense of accomplishment. They were standing on Austrian soil. It felt liberating. They were happy, loud, and boisterous—eager to reach their goal, now so near.

VII

General Ruska bit the quill so hard it cracked.

Count Piatti, the supreme commander of the 7th Corps, had just arrived in Hermagor at the head of his men, and went directly to see Ruska.

He was outraged. It wasn't enough that the flight of the young men fit for military service had hit him like a bolt from out of the blue. That was merely the first shot full of dark foreboding that had struck him in the head. He was furious that the interrogations yielded nothing—the locals were as obstinate as beasts, staring obtusely at the ground as if incapable of thought. Following the advice of Maroni, who often offered useful advice, he hadn't made it into a huge affair. He also thought this was the smartest course of action, although it was by no means satisfactory. Sensitive to each incoming sign, at first he expected an imminent catastrophe. Maroni knew how to calm him down and quickly make him see the absurdity of asking for help from headquarters when there wasn't yet the slightest indication of any serious counterattack by the enemy.

Maroni seemed to be right, and this somewhat pacified Ruska, but this didn't keep him from searching for those who had fled. It was immediately obvious to him that they had gone to join the latest gathering of Austrian troops and he was pleased to have his conjecture confirmed.

In this new period of stasis, summer was fading more and more, and the first day of September arrived as a harbinger of decline, re-awakening the general's gloomy sentiments. The yellow and brown leaves had scarcely fallen to the ground in a glorious tiger-stripe pattern, but the very word "September" heralded the new season and set him brooding over the fact that no year could avoid its fall and decline.

He was grateful, though, for the news he received on that first day of the month, unpleasant as it was. The Austrian troops were at the border, ready to attack. The general composed himself, relayed the requisite communications to headquarters, and emphatically requested the additional troops necessary to counter the impending attack. At other moments, his agitation returned, which he re-kindled into a fury of hatred and rage. He plagued his subordinates to calm himself down. This was part of his nature, which surfaced in moments of stress, as a way of clearing his mind for more important decisions. He was also the type of person who finds a petty insult much more irritating than a significant defeat and so responds with all the hatred they can muster. The general was still injured by the memory of the waitress in the Unterberger inn—it was like a thorn in his side. It often began to sting, intensifying his outbursts, which the army knew well, but even Ruska's calmer moods unsettled the newly arrived Count Piatti, a man filled humanity's ideals.

This intimate exchange was preceded by an objective assessment of the directives and preparations for the near future, when the generals would be required to work closely together. Count Piatti would take the next day to move into the Upper Gail Valley to reach the border as quickly as possible. Ruska, meanwhile, would hold his troops in reserve, readying themselves to attack at a moment's notice. Only Hauptmann Maroni and a small number of foot soldiers would stay behind as the occupying force.

While pondering his military strategy, Ruska completely chewed through his quill. He spat as he threw it on the ground, then summoned Maroni. He communicated what was most important, in a tone that was more tense than he usually used with the captain.

Maroni received his orders with cheerful equanimity. He would've agreed in any case quite apart from the fact that subordinates are in no position to have their own opinions about orders, especially bad ones. So he was pleased to stay behind in Hermagor, even though he had a strong desire to move on and undertake something new. He did feel slightly wistful, but he consoled himself with the thought that he hadn't missed any major events so far, and besides, he'd never arrive too late, since wars never end as quickly as they begin—and with that, he took his leave from the general.

Ruska kept brooding for some time. He considered all the possibilities and for the first time was struck by the thought that until now he'd never thought in terms of victory and defeat—nor did he this time either. He'd only ever accepted success as the self-evident outcome after the fact. At the same time, it seemed senseless to weigh various possibilities—for in order to win, you must see victory not as something extraordinary, but as an absolute given, and defeat as impossible. This was the sum of his philosophy.

He sat down at his desk to append his signature and did so with a forceful stroke of the pen worthy of Napoleon himself.

"But what if both sides—we here and the Austrians over there—think the same thing, that victory is assured? Then who wins, who is right?"

General Ruska chuckled softly to himself, and his small eyes ran contentedly over the sweeping signature.

One simply doesn't think such thoughts.

September was nearly halfway over. But it was still summer, as glorious as in the first threshing days. The fog still slept among the meadows, and it seemed to want to sleep there a while longer. The leaves clung firmly to the trees and laughed when the wind chased them. Oh, the time when they would drop was still a long way off. Nevertheless, within a few days, everyone would say that autumn had arrived.

This no doubt also occurred to Franz Brandstetter.

The stuffy air in the large stable was filled with voices. The student glanced up and looked at the others. They stood there just as he did, with bare chests and dirty trousers, and their hands, like his, were constantly rubbing thick black brushes over the horses' warm bodies. There was no comparison to the glamor of the Frimont Hussars seen riding along streets and roads, their heads held high in the wind and as if with hurrahs written on their faces.

Banter flew back and forth. Franz Brandstetter recalled the cheerful hours with his fellows, but there wasn't a single morning from which he hadn't woken with a start to see himself drowning in a sea of uncertainty. And in the last few days he hadn't felt the slightest joy. The little chapel tolled each passing hour as if to mock him, and every scorching ray of sun stabbed deep in his consciousness. Everything was sneering at him, screaming at him, reminding him that autumn is coming.

And autumn came. The black letters on the calendar were adamant. And in October he wanted to be—no, he needed to be in Vienna. He often rested his head on his arms, his eyes stung, and he felt as if they were burning back his rising tears. He felt completely numb, overcome with a fierce madness, as if all his hopes had been shattered. He'd firmly believed that the fighting would erupt today or tomorrow—that the time of the conflict had finally come once and for all.

And yet the days dragged on. At first he'd been captivated by a hundred small things that carried the charm of novelty. That was when the town's fugitives were welcomed with cheers and given their assignments. The student, whose peculiar circumstances were kept secret, was assigned to Rittmeister Johann von Biró von Csik-Pálfalva's Frimont Hussars. The others, whose riding skills were minimal, were assigned to the 53rd Infantry Regiment, which was only partly deployed. Later, it would be augmented with the Szekler Border Regiment and placed under the command of Obristleutnant de Mumb. It was no secret, even to the men in the lower ranks, that the commander of the combined forces was not actually de Mumb, but rather Freiherr von Pirquet, a man of singularly persuasive influence. Although only a captain in rank, he commanded the 8th Jäger battalion as well as the Rittmeister's hussars, but his superiors could easily have entrusted him with something greater.

He had large, light-colored eyes that were friendly but could also flash with scorn. There were many who pretended to hate him, but who actually loved him. They called him a dirty dog who wanted to squeeze out every last drop of blood from them and who ought to be shot. But they probably sensed that they weren't capable of this, and so went back to groveling, eating out of his hand when he was gracious, and trembling at his unspoken scorn. He had a way of behaving that would have outraged arrogance itself. Still, there'd been battles in which everyone maneuvered to be near him, in which their lives hung on a judicious word from him. And it was the captain who intuited something of the student's character.

Brandstetter had reported to him along with his friends, giving him a list of their names written in his hand. Pirquet glanced at it and asked who'd written it. The student stepped forward not knowing what to expect. Then he felt one of the captain's looks for the first time, a look that could never be called indifferent. On another day, before Brandstetter was separated from his friends, part of the troop stood in rank and file, the new recruits doing their best to keep up. Pirquet was strolling across the field with de Mumb. Suddenly he stopped, gestured with his hand, and looked into Brandstetter's eyes.

"The bumpkins can write well," he said loudly and clearly.

The student flushed to the roots of his hair. He was afraid he would be interrogated and discovered. But nothing happened then and nothing happened later. Franz calmed down. Pirquet didn't give him another look, but Franz Brandstetter was moved to admire the man's powers. Nonetheless, he was careful not to mention this to his comrades.

At first, even the most recent events seemed as if they'd happened a long time ago; they flitted timidly through Franz's memory like an incredible fairy tale, but with each day that passed since leaving home they drew closer and became more real. Thoughts of his father began to preoccupy him more and more. After waking up on his first day away, the confrontation with his parental home seemed unavoidable. Yet he strove to find a conciliatory outcome as he imagined various versions of his future.

As understandable and justified as his father's anger might be, why should it be beyond reconciliation? Almost all the young fellows from the villages and market towns had left their work and their families and had joined the fight. Why shouldn't he be allowed to as well, especially since he'd been coerced into joining? All the others had forced him into it with their views—a view that they also shared with his father.

With these and other reflections he reassured himself, but not completely. He knew there was a flaw in his reasoning.

Out of a certain inhibition, he kept himself from thinking about Fini. He often pretended that she'd never come into his life, perhaps because he knew it had no place for her. He thought of other solutions, but after much varied reflection, the plain impossibility of their being together remained. He had to stifle every hope of being with her because he was determined to return to Vienna, even though he was growing more and more desperate by the day since the onset of the war seemed to constantly recede. Nonetheless his hope, this practically insane hope, increased with his despair.

On top of that he developed a new trait. From the rowdy, raucous soldier's life he'd just entered, he would retreat into the most secret, the most beautiful hours of an earlier time. The quiet pleasures of his first student years had gotten lost in the frenzy of the ones that followed. Now, in his brief moments of free time, he would sneak away to the chapel at night, or to hidden nooks during the day. There he nourished his desire, for which he unlocked the expanse of the cathedral, and called forth the dreamy semidarkness, the cool vault, the chill of the cold stones that gnawed through his knee bent in humility. He didn't pray, he neither wished nor requested anything. He was too consumed by his dreams, the pleasure of dreaming. He breathed in all his longing with the veiling smoke of incense and candles, while an incorporeal music enchanted his senses, its notes carried by the voices of somber choirs, and then by the power of the organ. The pleasure was increased by the shudders running through his body, sparked by the cold of the stones and his own excitement. He felt feverish from all of these sensations, and the icy jolts that shot through him from time to time dissolved into the pleasant fatigue that comes from extreme physical exertion and automatically brings contentment.

Now this thought was unpleasant, alien, and incomprehensible. It was hard to remain serious when he caught his mind drifting, his daydreams washing over him while he was supposed to be rubbing down a horse and was surrounded by his comrades' guffaws. In these moments, as he emerged from these reflections, Franz Brandstetter was hurt because he assumed their laughter was at his expense. This was also surely due to the fact that he knew he was not very well liked.

He was about to let his thoughts get away from him again. Summing up his feelings and ruminations, he quickly drew the nicest, most pleasant conclusions, and he was gripped by a realization that had never occurred to him before: suddenly he was convinced that everything would reach a happy conclusion if only he had the strength to escape this imposed fate, to break the bonds that kept him here, and thereby save himself at the last moment.

Who had the right to startle him from his calm, to chase and hound him from one unwanted course of action into another? At first he had hadn't been courageous enough to resist and release himself, but he was brave enough today to take the decisive step, no matter how difficult, even if it meant breaking his word, in order to find himself again.

The thought of breaking his word distressed him, but he had to escape. Tomorrow—or even better, today. He had to get away from this place, whatever the cost. He had only one life to lose but he valued the worth of his soul more than that of his body and so he was resolved.

It would have been better if the war had started early and finished quickly, he thought bitterly. But that was not to be. He was probably fated to choose between two paths. Choosing the right one was agony.

The decision to act lifted much of his burden. He smiled with relief, but his lips twitched with uncertainty.

Hauptmann Pirquet stepped into the doorway and looked around, his eyes unaccustomed to the semidarkness. His first glance, which the boys did not see but merely felt, made them look up. He waved them over, gave them a kindly look, and said it would be better for them to stop grooming and prepare themselves to ride by evening.

They remained silent. The student was deeply alarmed by this new surprise. When the captain had gone, the hussars broke into wild howls of joy. They punched each other and roughhoused, full of boisterous laughter. They were overjoyed. Now it was certain that the war would begin. Their order might be ambiguous, but they were finally set into motion.

No one had noticed that Brandstetter didn't join in the general rejoicing. He was bitter. He'd wanted to take the next step, but fate blew, with mocking cheeks, and was sweeping him farther, farther than he had ever intended. Of course Pirquet's remark implied that the war would begin. He'd waited for weeks, waited and waited, but events followed a different path. Only today had he resolved to close this phase of his life. He'd struggled for weeks, and now, at the very moment he'd made up his mind, it was wrenched away from him.

He went back to the horses and randomly stroked their thick, gleaming coats. The smell was suddenly unbearable—he sought freedom through the broad stable door.

It hardly seemed necessary to escape now. But despite the outbreak of war, everything might still be too late, for it was late.

Night had fallen. They were indeed riding. The infantry was far behind them but driven by the same enthusiasm. As soon as their horses' hooves struck the border, a single shout burst from the men: "For God and Kaiser, victory or death!"

The words echoed off the nearby cliffs and faded in the distance.

In the center of the throng was the student, Franz Brandstetter, who automatically mumbled the cheer along with the others. His thoughts were elsewhere. He was forced to consider that it was for the soldiers' enthusiasm that he'd abandoned his life and thereby lost it.

It was incredible—the French were actually fleeing.

The Austrians swiftly drove Count Piatti's troops before them, like they were running down game. They didn't allow themselves to catch their breath. Franz Brandstetter had to stay behind in Weissbriach with some wounded men. He was relieved when he heard the order because the thought of approaching Hermagor had made him tremble. He plainly acknowledged that he would've been incapable of going home so precipitously. Sooner or later, he knew that he would need to return, given their all but certain victory, and he began to prepare himself. His unpleasant emotions increased when he thought of Dean Freneau, but he forced himself to be cheerful and lighthearted.

Meanwhile, Obristleutnant de Mumb and Hauptmann von Pirquet had brought their men to just outside Hermagor with relatively few losses. Here, a brief battle broke out, in which the Austrians' favorable position on a hill gave them an advantage; they kept the upper hand before taking Hermagor without resistance. Hauptmann Maroni was grazed by a shot and refused to acknowledge the wound—he thought it was just a scratch. Nevertheless, he was unable to carry out his mission of staying in the market town. Along with General Ruska, he was one of the last of the French to leave Hermagor. The general didn't surrender, instead wanting to establish a connection with the occupying forces located to the south in Villach. He refused to give anything up.

With great joy, the local population saw Austrian soldiers again for the first time in years. The farmers were proud of their sons among them. Brandstetter was nowhere in sight, but his mother ran up to the soldiers and asked after Franz. She was very unhappy that he wasn't with them, but they comforted her by saying he was doing well and would follow soon.

During this time, an incredible incident took place in the parish house.

Shortly after the Austrians arrived, De Mumb and Pirquet entered the dean's residence, and Freneau eyed the officers with some astonishment. He smiled briefly and did so more broadly when Pirquet, with a wordless bow, handed him a sheet of paper, which he rapidly scanned.

"I am at your service," Freneau began gravely and Pirquet gave him an inquiring look.

"I hope, Reverend Father," the Obristleutnant replied, sheepishly and awkwardly, "that you do not misunderstand us. Our only task involves the decree … hmm … that is, we are set to deliver the government's decree to you. I find it personally extremely unpleasant … hmm … Reverend Father, to ask you … hmm … to place yourself under my … hmm … protection."

De Mumb looked helplessly at Pirquet. He didn't feel up to the embarrassing situation. Dean Freneau took a deep breath, carelessly wrapped the important document around his finger, and said in a deadly serious tone:

"To put it clearly: the government is of the opinion that dangerous traitors to the country must be made harmless. I, of course, share this opinion, consider myself charged, and am ready to submit myself to the verdict of a commission."

The Obristleutnant noted the scorn. "The Reverend Father is jesting, of course," he stammered.

"Reverend Father does not jest," Pirquet said coldly. He then turned to the door, opened it for his superior, and turned back again. "I request, then, that from this moment on you accept the protection of my men."

Outside, as the two officers crossed the marketplace, Pirquet turned to the other and, completely disregarding the preceding scene, said: "In my opinion, our victory is by no means decided. I suggest we strike again and force Ruska into battle."

De Mumb was somewhat reluctant to do this. He was satisfied to have retaken half the valley without too much trouble, and yet he realized it was by no means over. His response to Pirquet was emphatic: they should gather their forces to await the counterattack. Hauptmann Pirquet remained reserved and determined. Finally, they agreed that Pirquet would move south with some of their troops.

This, however, did not keep the French from coming back with reinforcements two days later, pushing the Austrians to the Kreuzberg Pass, where they had launched their attack and recaptured Hermagor.

As they retreated, the Austrians took Dean Freneau with them. They gathered at the border, where they segregated the wounded and had them transferred across the Drava Valley. Before Freneau was carted off, accompanied by his guards from the assembly point, Franz Brandstetter spotted him. The student was shocked and thought his heart had stopped. He didn't understand the circumstances of their reunion, but it was horrible for him. For a moment their eyes met. Then the student turned slowly away, feigning indifference, as if he hadn't even noticed Freneau. He took a few rapid steps up to a small wooden hut. There he stopped and felt his burning forehead. He wasn't any calmer and he couldn't resist the urge to look at the priest again. Keeping his head close to the wall, he peered in the direction he'd come from. Some distance away, Freneau was still standing, hesitant to climb onto the cart. He was smiling, and his eyes rested on the spot that Franz had fled. Franz looked at that smiling mouth and saw pity, superiority, and ridicule ... But it was a mild, bitter melancholy.

On the following day, September 18, 1813, the Austrians again set out from the Kreuzberg Pass. A fierce battle was fought at Weissbriach. Every man, French or Austrian, felt that this day would be decisive. The Austrians suffered the first losses, but they advanced little by little. At Möschach, the tide seemed to turn but, in the end, luck remained on the Austrians' side. As had been decided, Hauptmann Pirquet split off from the main body of troops and led a small detachment of his Jäger battalion into the woods and to the higher elevations of the Ach Forest on the left, then over Radnig and down the rift valley to cut off the enemy's retreat from Hermagor.

As they watched the French fleeing through the market square, the Hermagorers could hardly suppress their joy. On the general's orders, the occupying garrison also quickly prepared to march out.

At the inn, Hauptmann Maroni packed his things. He paced back and forth somewhat pointlessly while his men waited outside. He went into the kitchen. The waitress was alone.

"Yes, Fini, things are one way today, tomorrow another. Maybe we'll be back here tomorrow."

She looked at him in surprise. He sounded sad and hopeless.

"Yes, well," she murmured.

A pleasant smell came from the hearth.

"Ah, you're already cooking for your soldiers."

"I don't know," she said blushing in embarrassment.

"Yes, but I know," he said.

She lowered her head and thought a moment. Finally, she came to a decision and quickly prepared a pack of provisions for him. She handed it to him, her eyes full of doubt. He was moved and cheered up, thanked her, and gave her a kiss. She allowed it and watched him as he hesitated at the doorway, where he turned around twice, nodded, and then left.

Maroni abandoned the town with the last of the soldiers. The Austrians were not very far away. With victorious cries, they once again entered Hermagor. Some stopped for a short rest, while others, namely the Frimont Hussars under Rittmeister Biró and

Obristleutnant de Mumb's infantry, kept in pursuit. Near Obervellach another firefight ensued. In close formation, they pushed toward the town. Here, amid the tangling fighters, a bullet hit Maroni and shattered his knee, so that he fell into the grass on the side of the road. He briefly lost consciousness, then saw, as if through a veil, both friend and foe rushing past. The pain brought him back to, and he dragged himself a step farther and sought shelter behind a lone ash tree, which half concealed him. There he lay, his head awkwardly propped against the trunk, unable to think, filled only with the raging, senseless fury of pain.

As soon as the French had withdrawn, the farmers hurried out of their houses, the men more cautiously than the women, who frantically ran all over the place because they didn't want to miss their sons' return. With a grand gesture and show of patriotism, the mayor, Jakob Unterberger, cast off the title of *Maire* and took up the old one of *Bürgermeister*. He stood in the square with the townspeople and all eyes were drawn to him and his associates, full of curiosity. Their conversations augured coming changes.

And there they were, hot and still panting from exertion. The marching soldiers brandished their flags, creating a colorful picture that was instantly disrupted by the inhabitants' joyful frenzy. They crowded around the soldiers, laughing and weeping at once. It was all so sudden that no one understood exactly why they were so happy. The liberators were pulled into the houses, where the best smoked and salted meats, bacon and bread, and brandy and wine were waiting, spread out on the tables, to strengthen and restore them. Then inn was immediately filled with soldiers who were looked after like sons. Out of sheer gratitude, the Hermagorers couldn't do enough for them.

Franz Brandstetter was out of his saddle faster than any other. His horse was led away by many hands and so he was relieved of that task. He burrowed his way through the crowd, looking this way and that. The throng soon thinned, but even so, search as he might, he saw neither his father nor his mother. He didn't understand what was going on and what to do next. So he walked down the street, hesitantly, constantly looking back at the square. The gate to the house was open as always. He stopped for a moment before entering. The porch was silent and abandoned. But as soon as he stepped into the house, his mother clung to him, weeping loudly. She'd been standing close to the wall, so he hadn't seen her. He knew immediately that she had been waiting for him. He held her stiffly, but warmly. She pushed him to the table and sat him down on the bench, then took a seat next to him. She was still wiping her tears, blowing her nose, and sobbing. Finally, she began:

"Franz, Franz, the main thing is you're back. You're back and you're healthy." It was more lament than joy. He laughed. But she could not calm down. "If only you'd never left, my God, if I'd known, I'd never have let you go."

"But it's fine now, I'm back with you. And I'm healthy. Don't I look it?"

Yet she kept weeping, but he couldn't see why.

"Yes, and where's Father?" he asked.

Just as he said that, the farmer came in.

"*Grüss Gott*, Father." The student sprang up.

The old man hung a basket on a peg. He cast a brief glance at his son, then turned away and left, his shoulders slightly drooping. At the door he paused and looked back at his wife. "You, the cow's out of feed. Take care of it soon."

She sobbed again, louder than before, and the student could neither speak nor move. He'd often imagined this scene, and here it finally was, but the reality was more crushing than he could've ever imagined. He watched the farmer leave the house, then turned back to his mother, who sat collapsed on the bench, and said, more calmly than he'd thought possible. "If Father doesn't want me in his house, then naturally I'll leave."

He looked around him as if to imprint on his memory one last time all of the things he had loved for so long. He stiffened and walked out, then moved back up the street.

It hadn't been hard to say this and go. Only now did he completely grasp the enormity of the step he'd just taken. The very idea was hard to believe.

His feet were so heavy they seemed to sink into the ground and his mind was just as sluggish. He had no idea how often he had walked back and forth across the market square. Finally, he abruptly straightened his shoulders and entered the inn, going directly from the entrance hall into the large public room, which had only recently been filled with the French. It was bursting with people and noise. He first caught sight of Fini, who only had eyes for him. She came to him right away, beaming, and took his arm in both hands.

"Franzl ..."

"Hello, Fini," he murmured. She didn't know whether to laugh or cry. He told his friends to make room and squeezed in between them. He was distracted but tried to follow their conversations and join in.

The girl stood there a while, looking at him. His greeting left her confused. Franz Brandstetter didn't notice anything, he didn't seem aware of his peculiar behavior or the girl's dismay. No one at the table was surprised by his terse answers since he'd never chatted much with the soldiers. As she hurried past—there was more work than usual—Fini paused next to the student.

"Have you been to see your parents?"

"Yes."

"You didn't stay very long."

"We don't have much time. We want to keep after the French," he replied evasively, looking away again. She kept working, her thoughts troubled.

A few hussars stood up and called on all the others to press on.

"Let's keep running the French until they collapse—let's finish them off today!"

Others objected vigorously, claiming a short rest wouldn't hurt.

The Obristleutnant said nothing but secretly counted the minutes, making sure they would be able to reach Pirquet in time to avoid changing their course of action. Rittmeister von Biró went out into the street. He had no wish to stay indoors.

Franz Brandstetter had also risen from the table and spoke with Kaspar and the innkeepers. They, too, were surprised Franz hadn't stayed home any longer than he did.

"Well, what did your father say to his soldier?" Lisa asked innocently. The student thought they all knew his father's attitude, but it was possible they didn't. He pulled himself together and said with a laugh, "What else could he say?"

"That's right," the innkeeper said, filled with the importance of his fatherland's mission. But then they turned their attention to something else.

Fini emerged from the kitchen with a bucket to fetch water. Franz accompanied her to the courtyard without a word. He'd gradually recovered his composure and realized that they had more to say to each other.

"Were you all right the whole time?" the girl began.

"Yes," he replied.

She held the bucket under the stream of water that pelted the hard base of the container. The water rose and overflowed.

Neither said anything, but Fini did not yet leave. She awkwardly poured out some of the water.

"You look good," the student began again.

"Yes," she said.

He studied her closely. Her eyes were brimming with tears, but she contained them. He was deeply moved.

"Fini … did you think of me often?"

He didn't get a response. He swirled his hand in the trough.

"What did you think, about how things would go with us?" he murmured helplessly.

"I didn't think anything," she said, placing the bucket on the ground. She held her hands under the stream of water and it pushed them down.

"Didn't you ever think …" he began. And then, again: "If I only knew what to do."

94

Finally, he straightened up and grew more emphatic: "If only I didn't have to leave you here alone ..."

"I won't be alone," she finally replied, motionless.

"What do you mean?" he asked.

She was silent for a long time. Then she looked him: "Because I'm going to have a baby."

Fini was upset and the calm that had cost her so much effort turned into fear. She'd seen how her words had put him on edge. He first looked startled and confused. But then his changing expression frightened her, so she just looked at him, unable to speak or move. She didn't understand what was going on inside his mind. Only gradually did she notice the dark rings around his eyes, the fine wrinkles that looked so out of place on his youthful skin and underscored the unhealthy glare in his eyes. He was so stooped over and off balance that she thought he would fall, but she didn't dare move any closer to him. Her perceptive heart had a vague sense of this person's pain, but she felt free from any blame, since she'd never imagined interfering with the life he had planned. But now she wished she had never told him. She had worked hard to overcome her fear and although she would've liked to receive his support, she ended up offering him hers. She grabbed the full bucket and went up to the student.

"No one will ever know. It will only be between you and me. I promise. I always knew I could never be with you," she said softly, lowering her head so that she didn't have to see his face.

He followed her meekly into the kitchen. They didn't know where to begin. She would've liked to stay by his side, even if she didn't know what else to say, but she had work to do and was needed everywhere all at once since she'd spent such a long time with him in the courtyard. She tried to stay in the kitchen but eventually had to go into the public room. She came running back right away:

"Franz," she cried breathlessly, "the others have already left."

It was true. Biró had ordered the Hussars to ride on. The infantry and the Obristleutnant had followed suit. Only a small group of soldiers stayed behind, but not a single cavalryman remained behind.

Brandstetter took the news indifferently.

"Don't you need to go with them?" Fini was desperate and spoke to him fervently. This shook him awake. He didn't know what to say but was suddenly overwhelmed with a sense of urgency: he decided to ride after the others. If he were quick, he could catch up to them near Obervellach. He was sure of it. Together they hurried to his horse. Staggering as if drunk, he climbed into his saddle and once again Fini worried he might fall. She would've liked to give him her hand, but only stroked the horse's neck. He smiled forlornly at her and finally uttered his first words: "I'll be back this evening." Then he raced off, small clouds of dust rising where the hooves beat the ground.

The wind flowing against him didn't cool the terrible heat of his body, instead it felt oppressive and made it difficult to breathe. The speed of his ride set his head spinning. The most disparate images raced feverishly past him. Between white patches of fog created by the headwind and his bloodshot eyes, he saw Dean Freneau's smile, his return to the family farm, and Fini, who would have a child. And then earlier images: the fellows riding to liberate the valley, himself among them, and earlier, when they'd asked if was joining them. He saw himself hesitate, sensed his helpless, smiling lips, his fear of saying yes and no all at once.

But this soon passed, leaving him with the latest development. What was it he wanted? ... Ah, the war may already have been decided today. Then he would return to Vienna as if this period of time had never happened. But there was still Fini. How ... she had said, after all, that there was nothing for him to do, that she would bear the child alone. But that was not right. He bristled at taking it so lightly ...

The stones were flying, and he noticed that his hands were no longer holding the reins but were clutching the horse's mane. The animal held its head ever more upright. He tried to do the same.

How ... if he could do better by Fini after all. He could take over the farm, the Brandstetter farm. There was no need for any Honditsch. But he should've done better by his father. This thought was no longer a new one ... as he clearly recalled.

He lost his hold of the horse. He yanked the reins hard, forced the animal to stop, and jumped down. He knew that the loosely cinched saddled had slipped.

It hadn't been long since the noise of the battle had left Hauptmann Maroni. His pain was so insane it defied understanding. His lips and tongue were raw with teeth marks, and his martyred senses were alert to every movement when the trot of a single horse made him sit up and take notice. He unconsciously reached for his gun, propped himself up, and looked out. Feverish and blurry, his eye was trained on the approaching Austrian, and he felt threatened when the figure leapt from his saddle. A wave of terror surged through him. Everything in him shouted: life! He lifted his gun, blindly aiming it at the enemy, his trembling finger on the trigger.

It was as though some knowing force drew Franz Brandstetter's gaze toward the captain: his grasp of the situation and his grip on his gun worked simultaneously in an instant.

Two shots rang out as one in the silence of the early afternoon.

The student Franz Brandstetter sank into the dust of the road. He died instantly.

Meanwhile the battle passed through the two towns of Obervellach and Untervellach. The Austrians were drawing ever closer to the French who'd had a head start. The terrain rose and fell over two small hills, then the blue of Pressegger Lake came shimmering out of the enormous stretches of reeds.

The sight of it filled the Obristleutnant with a fiery intensity. He stormed forward to the first row of gunners and urged them to increase their speed. His eyes were glued to the forest on their left as if he expected the decisive moment to come from somewhere inside of it. The French finally gave up the fight and turned to flee. They tried to hide behind single trees in the section of forest near the road. In their rush, it was useless trying to defend themselves. They had only one objective: to escape south to safety.

They didn't understand how the enemy was suddenly behind them. They were overcome with a crippling confusion. But the

Austrians understood, because at the French soldiers' backs were Hauptmann Pirquet and his small, brave band who'd covered the strenuous march around the French in very short order. The enemy side couldn't find its bearing. Helpless and terrified, they crowded together, fleeing from the barrels of the Austrian guns, then scattered. One group, under Ruska and Count Piatti, who recognized the hopelessness of their situation, managed with one final push south to break through the circle closing around them. But no other troops escaped, for the Jägers were on the hunt.

Then the French soldiers ran to the lake in a senseless bid to save themselves, but the hussars pressed hard behind them.

The wild ducks flew away, the reeds shook under the murderous fire of bullets. Crazed steps staggered, ran, raced into the damp meadows, fled into the reeds. The soft muck gurgled, air bubbles came welling up, and the next step was swallowed by the black, swampy maw.

Shrill screams mixed with the rattling gasps of the dying. Desperate struggles raged, here between man and man, there between water and man. Those who hadn't been hit by a bullet were claimed by the lake, an enemy that cannot be shot at, trod down, or strangled. The lake was more horrible than the unfettered human animals.

It lay calm and blue in the warm afternoon sun, mercilessly engulfing man after man. Over the water dragonflies played, gnats danced, while little spiders swam with wheeling legs.

Toward evening, Hauptmann Pirquet, having been stabbed three times with a bayonet, returned to the head of his men with all the captured flags, drums, and guns. The number of prisoners was large as well.

On the road between Hermagor and Vellach, they came upon the riderless horse. Not far away they found Franz Brandstetter. One of the men in the group also noticed the French captain. They all shuddered when they saw the cramped bodies and distorted faces. Maroni bore a second shot that had torn open his abdomen.

They brought the dead to the market town. Brandstetter's mother fell upon her son, her pain beyond measure. Vaba stood apart from the crowd and looked at the farmwife with contempt.

The farmer was nowhere to be seen.

On the road between Hermagor and Vellach, an old cross still stands today. It is called "The Honditsch Cross" because it was erected by Georg Wernitznig, the Honditsch farmer who later took over the Brandstetter farm. The commemorative plaque relates that an Austrian and a French soldier fell on this very spot on September 18, 1813.

The chronicle of Hermagor reports that the Illyrian Provinces, and with them the Gail Valley, were officially conquered in the Battle of Leipzig on October 17 of that same year.

A further report finds Dean Freneau years later back in the market town of Hermagor, serving as a priest, with no further mention of any grounds for suspicion.

Translator's afterword

Written in 1944 when Ingeborg Bachmann was eighteen, *The Honditsch Cross* is her second-longest completed prose work after *Malina*, yet it wasn't published until 1978. This historical novella, set in southern Carinthia in the summer and fall of 1813, recounts a minor battle during the final days of the Napoleonic Wars in French-occupied Austrian territory. The Honditsch cross of the title is an actual wooden cross in a wayside shrine erected in honor of fallen soldiers between the villages of Hermagor and Bachmann's father's hometown of Obervellach.

In 1943 and '44, her father, a lieutenant in the Wehrmacht, was stationed at the eastern front and her mother had relocated with her younger sister and brother to the safety of Obervellach during the Allied bombing of Klagenfurt. The teenage Ingeborg was living in Klagenfurt with several classmates and resisting pressure to join the Bund Deutscher Mädel, the girls' branch of the Hitler Youth, all the while frequently running to the bomb shelter. When home on leave in the summer of '43, Matthias Bachmann, who had always encouraged his daughter's literary aspirations, suggested she write a story about the history of that cross. The result was a work of fiction that reveals the sway the genre of the *Heimatroman*— the "homeland novel" that celebrates rural life, local traditions and dialects, attachment to the fatherland, and idealized pastoral landscapes—had over Bachmann at the time. More importantly, in foregrounding tolerance of the ethnic Slovenian minority and the

senseless waste of war, this novella also reveals the young writer's courage and independence of mind.

The nationalist fervor that spread through Carinthia under French occupation and brought about Franz Brandstetter's death echoes the rabid nationalism and racism rampant in the Third Reich. The National Socialists were intentionally fanning tensions between German and Slovenian speakers in Carinthia that remained from the 1920 plebiscite, in which 59% of Carinthians, the majority of whom were Slovenian speakers, voted to remain part of Austria rather than be annexed to Yugoslavia. In the early 1940s, Gauleiter Friedrich Rainer had been tasked by Berlin with implementing a "definitive solution" to the "minority problem" in Carinthia and Northern Carniola and had begun expelling ethnic Slovenians and handing their property to Germans. Against this backdrop, it is noteworthy that Bachmann would include, along with some "blood and soil" imagery of the traditional *Heimatroman*, passages mythologizing the Windish, a traditional name for ethnic Slovenes who were assimilated into the Austrian borderlands.

> The Windish live among ethnic German Austrians in the Gail Valley, as they do throughout southern Carinthia. They have their own language, which neither Slovenes nor German speakers completely understand. With their presence, they seem to want to blur the borders—the border of the country, but also of language, customs, and mores. They form a bridge, their pillars standing firmly and peacefully on both this side and the other. And it would be good if this were to remain forever the case.

What also keeps *The Honditsch Cross* from being a simple, romanticized *Heimat* novel is the way Bachmann complicates notions of nationality in her characters. While the Austrians are mostly portrayed as heroic and the French as arrogant and abusive, the two sides are not shown as simply black and white. Similarly, she includes the complicated Windish character Mateh Banul as emblematic of the rich hybridity of the Austrian population. This traveling peddler also serves as a sly, necessary go-between for the cultural groups.

In addition, Bachmann is—for such a young writer—surprisingly clear-eyed about the tacitly accepted norms of sexual exploitation in village life. Women at the bottom of the strict social and economic hierarchy were fair game and dispensable yet still subject to moral condemnation. It is also remarkable that she is able, as a teenager, to so vividly reimagine a small historical event. She richly fleshes out the blanks between the commemorative plaque of the Honditsch Cross and the lines of a chronicle she found in the Hermagor archives. Furthermore, against a backdrop of bombing raids and parades of Nazi soldiers in Klagenfurt, she created a story that commemorates the meaningless destruction of war as well as the futile deaths of the novella's two more honorable characters and its two ostensible heroes, Franz and the French captain Maroni.

Although this novella is far more traditional in style and structure than Bachmann's major prose works, it holds the seeds of themes that will preoccupy Bachmann for her entire writing life: the ethics of geographic and linguistic borders, the richness of transnational, multiethnic and multilingual communities that resist nationalist and racist tendencies, peripheries as a beneficial, anti-ideological force, the loss of childhood idylls, the ways in which violence against women frays the social fabric, and a utopian nostalgia for the House of Austria. *The Honditsch Cross* offers a snapshot of an engaged, rigorous, and innovative writer emerging from her chrysalis.

I'm deeply grateful to Philip Boehm, who has been translating and retranslating Bachmann for decades, for his patient and painstaking advice. While his editing has enormously improved my translation of *The Honditsch Cross*, all mistakes and infelicities are mine alone. My thanks also go to Barbara Epler and Tynan Kogane of New Directions for their dedication to literature and the writers and translators who create it.

TESS LEWIS